IT ALL STARTED WITH A FEW RUMS

By George Jobb

ABOUT THE AUTHOR

Written by his son Brandon. My father, by profession is a semi retired commercial truck mechanic. He has loved listening to and telling stories throughout my life. As part of his profession he had written thousands of one line and single page descriptions of work-related repairs. Mostly true, some embellishment and a few lies. Can you believe that? A mechanic that lies about the work that was done and charged people for.

George Jobb has worked a variety of jobs since the age of 14; such as waiter, busser, cook, mill worker, diamond driller, plumber, truck driver, reserve soldier, self employed, commercial truck mechanic, truck shop owner, commercial diver, and skipper.

He has been a lifelong practitioner of martial arts with 25 years of amateur competitions. He holds a 3rd degree black belt in Judo. Sustaining such injuries as: 6 dislocated shoulders, 3 broken ribs, 1 dislocated knee, 1 herniated disk, numerous broken toes and at one time had trouble wiping his own ass. As well, he holds a 1st kyu brown belt in Shotokan Karate, 3 years of Brazilian Jiu Jitsu and a year of amateur boxing from which he still admits he does not like being punched in the head, but who does? His highest level of competition was 3-time medalist at the World Judo Masters. Placing first in Tokyo Japan in the 100kg - 40 to 45-year-old division in 2003.

He has owned, fixed, bought and sold and ridden motorcycles since the age of 14 and still rides today.

He is a brash yet highly rational and intelligent person. He has been a strong father figure for me throughout my life. Although this is not a bibliography, his words and ideas convey the man he was and will continue to be until his death. This is his story.

PREFACE

Authors Note: *This is a story of two motorcycle trips done by myself throughout my life. The first trip was solo in May 1986 on a Suzuki GS1100ES at the age of 26. That was when I met self for the first time on a deserted stretch of Baja Hwy. This trip started in White Rock, British Columbia. I rode through the United States, down the Baja, to La Paz Mexico. I then cut across the Sea of Cortez by ferry, killing a man along the way to Mazatlán, Mexico. I hung out and drank to much along with having some great sex for a couple of weeks before returning home. As best I can recall the length of the trip was about 4 weeks.*

The second trip was started in October 2018 from Abbotsford, British Columbia to San Jose del Cabo which is at the farthest tip of the Baja Peninsula. Meeting another version of myself along the way. It was done on a R1150GS BMW at the age of 58 with a friend. This story was written based on true events, some embellishments and a few lies. It is also a bit of an instruction manual if you haven't had great sex in a while.

CHAPTER 1: THE BEGINNING OF THE ROAD TRIP

Abbotsford BC, 2018 - I had been thinking of a road trip to the Baja for some time. Chief "his nick name", rather then Richard Tomas had been following a group on Facebook that had planned to head down south in October. Meeting a group in San Diego, CA then zig zagging by motorcycle through the Mexican Baja, destination La Paz.

I previously done the trip solo in the 80's. Leaving White Rock BC a few days after Expo 86 started. No GPS back then boy. Just some travelers' checks, US cash, a map and a compass. It's just one road north south the Trans peninsular Highway. One wouldn't expect to get lost, but better safe than sorry. I should mention I had no tool kit or spare tire tube at the time. Just a 1983 Suzuki GS1100ES.

MARCH 1986 - The trip would take many days, and it's necessary to stop periodically. The first night, after crossing the US border, I stopped in the mountains of southern Washington or northern Oregon. There was a small turn off the I5. One small hotel sign. It pointed along towards a winding road which ran alongside a river in a forested area. Gave me the urge to go fishing. Came up to the hotel not far down the road. It was a house with some bungalows attached to it. Very rustic Ma and Pa type place, nice people. Looked like it was set up for fishermen. Nice enough rooms with a small kitchenette and comfortable bed. I unloaded my stuff and headed to the restaurant bar down the road. I had a burger and fries, played some pool and chit chatted with the locals. Kind of an odd group. I met one educated native Indian guy, reminded me that the US and Canada were at war in 1812. I informed him my ancestors did not arrive from Ireland until 1837 and that they did not own slaves either. He seemed to like that and smiled. The barmaid was giving me the eye. She was a bit, well worn with a few extra pounds. There was also this older dude, probably in his thirties. Kind of the burnt-out salesman type. I drank till at least 11 or 12 o'clock - playing pool and bull-shitting, then headed back to the motel for a good night's sleep.

Even in the 80s the I-5 was a busy highway. It runs through Seattle, Everett, Portland and it is a bit of a boring drive, was good to get past that. Southern Oregon is scenic with less traffic. Heading out of the mountains, always is a big deal. It dry's up and the humidity drops as the valley begins to open up. Just a different feel when you're on a bike. You notice the vegetation change and the different smell when your riding a motorcycle. These are greats roads, good visibility, signage, and banked corners fair for high speed driving. Some one must have thought things through. There're quite a few rest areas in either direction. Some of them in those days would have volunteers with coffee and sandwiches for travelers. Not sure who paid for it at the time. It was nice. Bathrooms were clean. I never had any problems, but I'm sure some people do.
There were good places to stop and stretch a bit. I'd pull out the map and check the mileage and estimate the distance and time between where I was and where I was going. Always re-evaluating where to spend the night.

The second night I stopped in Bakersfield. If you've never been there, compared to the Pacific Northwest it's flat and dry, back then it was just one and two storey buildings. Not much to look at. By 7 or 8 o'clock I had had dinner and wanted a beer. So, I asked the front desk guy Byron if there was local pub or bar close buy. He pointed me down the road, it wasn't too far away. Half a mile or so. I hopped back on the bike found the bar and parked. The parking lot seemed empty. It was a big building, I walked in the front door and was greeted by a 6-foot 4 cowboy: with mustache, cowboy hat, and big old belt buckle. I'm guessing he was one of those urban cowboys. I remember him kind of eyeballing me. You know staring at me. I asked,

"are you open?"

He paused for about 2 or 3 seconds before answering. Not all cowboys do this, but quite a few. Every time you ask them a question, god fucking knows why, but they would take 2 or 3 seconds to answer. It always irritated me. Finally, he goes,

"Yup."

Then another 4 seconds before asking if I was coming in. Meanwhile I'm looking around at the room. Its big. Probably room for 200 or 300 people. Maybe more if they're standing. Except not a single fuckin' person in there. Just him, me and a guy behind the bar. I asked him if it would get any busier. Now he's really glaring at me. 4 seconds later,

"yup" and a nod and, "yup" again.

Ok, then so I'll go in and have a beer, take my time. Should be someone to play a game of pool with or check out the local girls. No one comes in, second beer another Budweiser, you couldn't get drunk if you drank twenty of them. Two hours go by and I'm still the only fucking person in the place. So, I walked back up to door man, said I'm thinking about leaving. Does he know of any places that are happening? Another 3 second delay... He says,

"what do you mean?"

I say,

"like a night club, you know, like maybe where there's

women, or a band, dancing the normal stuff?"

Cowboy was maybe 30, I'm not sure why he didn't understand what I was asking. He's staring at me and goes "yup, there a place down the street. Can't remember what it was called." A few more seconds go by and I asked what it was like. He said,

"some crazy shit goes on there." Just like that. Still staring at me, glaring.

I'm not sure if he's challenging me or he's retarded. I end up leaving, driving down to the next place.

It was something out of 1978, they still thought they were AC/DC at the peak. Long hair and heavy metal music, which I can't stand. Now I'm getting more looks from the locals, like there were the cool kids on the block and I'm the new kid. To me it looked like a bunch of throwbacks. I try to get a little chit chatty with the girls, but it wasn't working. I lasted about an hour and left. To this day, I still think of Bakersfield as a shit hole full of retards. It would take a lot to change my mind. I had a neighbor who grew up in Stockton in the 50s and 60s, which is close to Bakersfield. He also said it was a complete shit hole. I've ever only met one other person who had been there. He said it was a total a shit hole too, so to all you too sensitive urban cowboys, fuck you.

The next stop was Long Beach, CA. My parents insisted that I stay with my aunt, or second aunt. I'm not sure what the blood line was. She had a bungalow near Los Angeles in Long Beach.

She was a widower; her husband was in the US navy most of his life. He was an engineer or mechanic on submarines. I had met them up North a few times. Nice people, he was a bit controlling maybe judgmental? They had spent a few days with my parents. At the end of the second day, of that visit he had admitted that he wasn't sure about me. But after watching me on a heavy bag in the backyard he thought I was alright. In my late teens and early 20s I wasn't one to take advice. I was more likely to tell an old man to get the fuck out of my way. I didn't this time, just nodded. I did find a nice clean golf shirt in the laundry. I wore it out that night, it fit pretty good. He asked about it in the morning. I guess it was his. I shrugged and said I'd put it back in the wash. Ya, who's the big dog? My aunt Evangeline was a very nice lady, mature, sophisticated, I was looking forward to having a visit with her. It was agreed to spend two nights with her.

So, I got to within a few blocks of where she lived and phoned her from a gas station. I had not been to Long Beach before, but it's a nice area. The guys at the gas station were staring at me when she pulled up in her Cadillac. Now they were staring at her and me with a smile on their faces. A young guy in his 20s down to visit with his aunt. Hmm… I can imagine what they were thinking. I followed Ante back to her place and she showed me my room.

I asked her if there was anything I could do around the yard or house. She got me out washing her car. I washed it to Canadian standards. It rains a lot up here so it's usually a quick job, before it starts raining again. She came out, looked at it and told me to redo the rims. Ya Californian women, even in her 50s she was still pretty feisty at the time.

She fed me a good meal, I went to bed early that night. I had put in eight or nine hours on the sport bike, that's a pretty good ride. I only had one full day to spend with her. So, she took me to the Spruce Goose. The old Howard Hughes plane that was on display in the harbour at the time, there were tours on it. Its was an interesting story behind the build. We did the walk around and then headed over to the Queen Mary, the old ocean liner that had been decommissioned and berthed there, now used as a lunch restaurant. She took me there, as a gentleman, I was holding her arm as we went on to the ship into the restaurant area. The maîtred eyed us both, he was about my age. With a big smile on his face he took us over to a table and sat us down. Evangeline smiled and said, "I think he thinks we're a couple." I nodded, I got that impression also. So, we kind of hammed it up a bit and flirted over lunch. It was a lot of fun. She was a great older gal. Well, to my surprise, that night she had a date. That evening while kicking back after mowing the lawn I decided I needed a jog.

Evangeline thought that was a good idea. I was young and fit at the time. I circled the block, ran out of the neighborhood she lived in and headed out to the main road. Looped around checking things out and wondering why every backyard beside the sidewalk had a six-foot concrete fence. I thought that odd. But if I had to, I could probably jump it pretty quick. Hands up top and swing the legs over. I thought I heard something behind me. I look and there's a police car. Their trailing me, hmm... There was a colored guy and a white guy. I was used to things up North. I stopped, they stopped. I walked over and asked them what there doing? Well they asked what I was doing. I said, "I'm out for a jog." Well at that time, in the mid 80s people didn't go out for jogs in that area. It was a fairly main road I was on. First, they asked if I was from around there? They were kind of smiling. I said no I wasn't, I was from up North and was just visiting my aunt for a couple of days. Still smiling they asked, "and you're just out for a jog hum." I said "ya ya." "Well there's half a dozen drive by shootings a week around here" was the response back. I said I hadn't noticed anything suspicious, except people giving me odd looks. They smiled and nodded, asked how much further I was going. So, these two guys, good guys followed me along for the next couple of blocks until I turned back into the subdivision. Another nod and they were on there way. It was good to see the local police were keeping an eye out for its citizens back then. That was more than enough in one day for me.

Back at Evangeline's place, when she came out of her bedroom. I was like hmm, not bad looking for an older gal. White skirt on, red top, a little lipstick, not over done. Not a bad rack on her either for her age. Now that surprised me, normally in my 20s I didn't eye up older women to much, but she wasn't looking to bad at all. I mentioned that she cleaned up pretty good. She kind of smiled and maybe even blushed a bit. Anyways I was fast asleep before she got home. I headed off the next day. To cross the border. She said to make sure I stopped in on my way back through. Oh ya.

Now going through Tijuana in '86 was something else. Hard to put into words, but I'll try. First, it's holy fuck what is this, I'm going to die. The first main intersection I came to be some kind of five corners of chaos. Never seen anything like it. Cars, buses, people all rushing in honking, waving, smiling, and yelling all at the same time. I swear they all knew each other and were putting on some sort of show. I mean, was this even real? It all took about three or four seconds to process. Then I thought, just as well give it some throttle and to see what happens. A space opened up and I was through the worst of it. After that, there was what looked like a three-mile strip mall of every type of business you could imagine and some I couldn't. Sort of like what I imagined Shanghai looked like at the turn of the century. Or a side street in Morocco. A lot funnier now. Though I was shitting my pants at the time. Is this what it's going to be like the whole 1200 miles? Holy fuck. After about an hour of heading south, traffic started to clear.

At that time the old highway connected with the new one about five km north of Ensenada. This was one of the nicest roads I had ever driven on at the time. Ocean on the right, rolling hills on the left, lots of curves and banked corners. There wasn't much traffic, so I pulled over into a viewpoint to take it all in. The pull off was empty but paved and maintained. I wasn't there two minutes before a police car pulled in. He obviously had followed me and was considering whether or not to rob and murder me. I had only been in the country and hour and I thought I was going to die. He got out of his car which had a machine gun mounted in the middle and walked towards me. He was smiling and nodding, He's probably is going to shoot me up close and push me off the edge, then steal my motorcycle. He says "hello" and starts looking at the bike. Hmm. He then said he used to race motorcycles professionally in Mexico City. The same Suzuki 1100 was the bike he used. I was impressed, we talked for a while. He got back into his car and headed South. I caught up with him on the highway a few minutes later. He waved me beside his car and gave me the rev-it-up signal with a smile. I nodded and scooted past him. That was an OK guy.

I probably should have stopped in Ensenada and thought things through a little more, but like a true jackass Gringo I pressed on. You know to this day, I still think locals knew I was a newbie. Ya I know, Mexicans do have a sense of humor as I've learned over the years. It is possible there's some sort of collective conscious and this Baja'ers were all just fucking with me. I've had this happen years later there when I was rude to someone or had gone out of my way to help or given a ride to someone that was standing on some back-desert road. There's probably another story there.

The road settled down and I got back into my rhythm. I pushed on another twelve hours through rural farm and ranch land and the odd dusty town. I end up my first night in Guerrero Negro. That's about half way down the Baja, just a mile or so north of the 28th parallel.

Oh, I forgot to mention stopping for lunch. Now, I know that sounds easy in a small town, about a block long and half a block wide. But not when there's an election going on it isn't. An election in smaller towns in Mexico looks like something between a circus and a Baptist sermon. You ain't at the front of any line that day, week, or month. Chances are you'll be queued up for half a block. No signs either, no sir! Why would you need signs in a small town anyway right? Everyone already knows where it is. You just ask, or in my case, because I didn't speak Spanish you just look for what looks like a restaurant. More than once walking into private homes by mistake. Which a lot of time their attached

to the restaurant anyway. It was hard to tell the difference. After a few wrong guesses, an older woman pointed me to a doorway.
 Across the street, things were looking up. Although the young waitress was a little distracted on account of the election. There was a man in the perfectly pressed white shirt pointing in the air and at people very sincerely. Obviously making many promises to anyone who believes. Kind of like politicians today. That's what was going on down the street a little further. How could someone be expected to serve some gringo lunch with all this going on.

After a few minutes of me pointing to my stomach along with the international shovel food in your mouth gesture. I wasn't sure food was on the way. What I got was a measured cup of rice, some black beans and what I was think was a piece of beef. The old school Mexican style beef, more like an old sole of a boot.

Wow! Tijuana driving and now beef like leather. Two firsts in one day. I was now concerned I might starve on this trip. Also, the waitresses gave me the nose up sign when I didn't smile at the food. Which kind of slighted me at the time. At twenty-six, up North, I was still considered a dude at the time. Tall, lean, and not bad looking. But it is what it is and the Irish Jew in me wasn't complaining about the buck fifty price. Shut up and eat up. Time to put on some more miles.

The ride into the town of Guerrero Negro was like riding into an old Clint Eastwood movie. Dusty brick and mortar buildings, dirt and sandy roads. Not a soul in sight. Just a three-legged dog laying on a doorstep. How could there possibly be that many three-legged dogs in Mexico? It's not much different these days either except there's now an Oxo in town.

I found a family run hotel. It was quiet and deserted, but clean and somewhat organized. Eleven dollars for a room. All good, well time to eat again. After a half hour discussion and pointing at the dinner menu. I think I ordered chicken, or a whore? I wasn't sure. But at four dollars I wasn't complaining. The debate also improved my pronunciation of the word, "Pacifico."

Being the only person in the restaurant at the time made me a little uncomfortable. Probably because it was not the proper time to eat dinner in Mexico. Gringos eat at 5 or 6 pm, Mexicans 8 to 10 pm. A few Pacificos later I was starting to relax. That's when the Montanans sat down and sure as shit they had rode in on bikes. Took me awhile to process this. It was not what I was expecting. It was one of those moments where things just feel too out of place to be real, and time lags a bit.

Well naturally, being the only gringos in town we sat together. Strength in numbers. They were two brothers and a friend all from Montana, all early 30s to mid 40s, the taxi driver who pointed them to the hotel also informed them that there was a whore house bar just outside of town and that we should give it a visit and he could show us the way. What could go wrong there? The three or five shots of tequila had made us all brave. The dinner ended up being fish and shrimp, quite filling and fresh. Although I would soon be introduced to the runs. Probably from lunch.

So off we headed on a dirt road, through a garbage dump about five miles east out of town. I was sure we were all going to die, there's no way this isn't a setup then, holy shit, an old brick bar type looking building dimly lit appeared.

In hindsight, that night we were probably on the edge or perhaps a little over. We walked inside, along with the taxi driver who was all smiles. The bar was dimly inside and out. There were a few tables, a long bar, and a bored looking bartender, who now starting to smile. Hmm, a few beers and more tequila and things were looking ok. Then a couple of women showed up out of nowhere. Well if you haven't met a Baja woman, they're not bad looking: fine features, on the lean side, nice hair and teeth, with shapely asses and a feisty spirit. According to locals it's because of their pirate ancestor blood. Some French, Spanish, Dutch, with a mix of Irish. Well these two weren't any of that, so I abstained, thank you. Not on any moral ground. I just wasn't drunk enough and they were ugly. Also, a bit doughy looking... as in pastry dough not deer doe. Don't worry, two out of three of the Montanans indulged. Ladies made some money.

Now, the younger Montanan spotted a stuffed iguana on the shelf behind the counter. He had spent the most money, on account he went for the full ride. So, some negotiations started on the purchase. Ten minutes later and more tequila it was his. Seven dollars, I think. Having no place to stow it. It was decided to tape it to the top of his helmet. Which took the efforts of four people and advice from eight. Looked ok, sort of. So, we all moved outside for a photo. Four gringos on motorcycles, one taxi driver, two whores looking quite happy with the night. I might add, and one bartender. Oh and a iguana taped the American's helmet. Two photos were taken. Never heard from them and lost mine, but it would be hard to make this shit up.

It's seems strange now, but there was a warmth both in the air and body on the ride back to town. Trusting strangers on a clear night in the desert. You know there's something about the desert at night, I'm an atheist but I'll tell you, it's hard to believe you're alone on a warm desert evening...

CHAPTER 2: PREPARATION SEPTEMBER

2018

After fourteen months of pulling wrenches in a truck shop and pushing fifty-eight years of age, I was due for a change. A road trip or any goddamn thing. The wife could tell I was starting to become miserable with the work, less enjoyment and drinking more. Time to, "make a move" so they say.

I confirmed with my Chief, I was in. Which of course made his wife happy, being at least as cheap as me. We could now split the hotel bills. I tried to talk him into tenting it or using hammocks on the road side. He didn't go for it.

I had tried out the hammock on a bike trip into Harrison Lake BC, a month earlier. Strung the hammock between two trees then tied a tarp over it. Worked ok. Lot of trees in BC. Not so many in the Baja as buddy pointed out. Now, a night in an empty un-serviced campsite an hour down a BC logging road should be pretty quiet. Except, all the critters that live there come out at night. There are so many! I could have sworn that there was a small army tromping around under the hammock and in the bushes most of the night. Which caused me to jump out of the hammock a few times, which is a feat in itself. Searching the perimeter with flashlight and machete in hand. Didn't find a damn thing. Although a few guys I told about this, afterwards, thought it was pretty funny.

I start preparing the bike. I had bought a used BMW 1150GS a few months earlier for $3400 Canadian. It needed a little work. Few dents in the tank. No problem. Handlebars slightly bent. A little uncomfortable on the right wrist, but manageable. A few small brake vibrations and squeaking noise. Actually, I lost rear brakes testing it off road, shortly after I bought it. I had shut the engine off and coast down a gravel logging road up on Vedder Mountain in the Chilliwack area. I wouldn't advise this on a 550 lb motorcycle with a 220lb driver and 130lb wife on the back. It carries a lot of momentum. The rear brakes overheated, and the front brakes don't work that well on loose gravel over hard packed till. It's called brake fade from overheating. Always remember to gear down while going downhill on a heavy bike. Good news, the compression was good, and I didn't dump it. Just a little piss on my pants.

So, I replaced the front and rear pads also put some fresh brake fluid in. Other then that, and a few rattles and ticks on the start-up, it all looked good. More or less.

The left side rattle was due to a cam chain tensioner. Eighty-five dollars and an easy hour install. Right side tick was something else. Tried valve adjustments, but no difference. I tried changing the cam pushrods on right side, but the ticking got even worse. Did some reading up on tick problems. Turns out the rocker tube hold down is adjustable and it was loose, specks say five thou. Tried adjusting it and no difference. It was time to phone up the BMW shop. So, there was also the transmission and differential oil changes. Oh ya, and headlight-low beam was not working. Just some loose wiring and getting to know the bike. Also repaired loose wiring on an extra set of LED driving lights. Just that goddam tick left.

More aggressive tires would be needed for the off road and sand of the Baja. I ordered them online, $211 Canadian delivered to the door. At the time I was putting them on in the third level of an underground parking, middle of August, was no fun. Cracking the rim bead on a ten-year-old tire was a bit trying. Once it popped, not to bad to swap the new knobby on. Oh, they looked good. Nothing like big old knobby on a big old bike.

I heard BCAA could supply an international driver's license. Thinking this was important, I decided to get one. Fifteen minutes and thirty-five dollars later I had a four by six inch - seven-page document in many languages. It looks quite hokey. I was reminded by the teller that I should still carry my Canadian driver's licence with me just in case. I didn't ask in case of what, but I have more than a few friends who have had their driver's licence taken for inspection and not returned in Mexico. So, it's easy to guess why.

I definitely have a few more back ups than I did in the '80s. Particularly in the tool area, including a flat tire repair kit and a hand pump. A little slow but lightweight and I'm not in a hurry. Wrenches, ratchet sockets, feeler gauge, spare valve stem, vise grip, test light and crimp connectors. Also, Silicon, JB weld, filter wrench, tie straps, lights, extra engine and trans oil. All this stuff mostly fits into two roll up pouches. After twenty-five years as a commercial transport mechanic, I just seem to carry around more shit. Both physically and mentally, not sure what to chuck out and what to keep.

Now for personal items; a hammock (which I was excited about). Not exactly sure why, but I think it's a good conversation piece and you can also sleep in it. Kind of like a multi purpose tool. A 6x9 tarp could be used for anything. Extra tie straps, clothes, wash and trim gear; older guys are hairy. Compass, map (still old school). I had thought about installing my TomTom GPS, but I don't know, it just seems like more shit to go wrong. You end up memorizing roads and names of towns when using paper maps. Also, you'll pay more attention to road signs. Kind of more engaging than just pumping out the miles with the GPS.

More stuff: camera, phone, tablet, some cash, (bank machines work fine in Mexico and the exchange rate is set daily), spare helmet, glasses for reading and driving. I tend to pack a good First Aid kit. You know tape, Polysporin ointment, gauze, Chlortrimeton, Advil, EpiPen, good bandages, and those butterfly strips to use as stitches. The reason why is, I once had a beetle the size of a golf ball hit me in the face shield at seventy miles an hour! I had to pull over to clean the visor, couldn't see a damn thing, yellow guts all over. I could see it coming from a quarter mile away. Like some drunk wandering down the center of the highway. Just couldn't dodge it. Actually, it was kind of mesmerizing. It was just strange. A small cut or scratch in a humid environment can get very nasty really quick. I once had a small mosquito bite on my ankle turn into a weeping open sore the size of a dime in three days. My ankle had started to swell, and I had a noticeable limp.

Look after your shit. The further you are going south, the more venomous the bites become. A sting from a wasp feels like someone sticking a nail in your back. A half inch high, three-inch diameter welt will form within minutes. That's from personal experience. Again, no simpatico down here. Don't wear bright clothing or the bugs will think you're a flower. They're not that smart. Fine to dress like a flower or plant in the city, but not when your off road. Yup, dress like the grey man or a homeless person. There're a reasons people sneaking around at night dress like that. They're hard to see. If your think I'm kidding have someone in white or colorful clothing stand by some bushes at night. It's like waving a flag. During the day in warmer climates it will attract the bugs. There just isn't much benefit from dressing nice and lots of down side.

CHAPTER 3:
GUERRERO NEGRO

1986 - Woke up a little hungover from last night's antics but felt full of life. I headed for the banjo, the runs had begun. I needed water. OK, I'm fine. Just a little loose. I have always found breakfast in Mexico to be pleasant. Not rushed. Eggs, tortillas, ham, and salsa, fresh orange juice and coffee, no rush. Well, only another trip to the banjo was rushed. The waiter who was now an old friend and also the bus boy from the night before was quite chatty. I paid the bill and was still chatting with the waiter and manager, possibly his father or uncle. It was mentioned that the young waiter wanted to go to La Paz, which was now a two-day drive by motorcycle. They asked if it was possible that he could get a ride with me. Now a 1983 Suzuki ES1100GE was a sport bike in the day. No luggage side carriers, small seat, small fairing, lean on tank type machine. My gear was in a hockey bag stuffed full. It was about one and half foot in diameter and 3 feet long. Slung over the back seat, tied down with bungee cords and 2 tie straps. Where did they think he was going to sit? I then noticed the luggage he was standing beside. He had already packed. Hmm, well I did not want to be rude, but this was not going to work. You really don't want to insult the most influential family in town. "Lo siento buddy", But it is not possible to drive 800 miles with another person on top of my luggage, we would be sure to die. OK, we thought we would ask. "Good day."

A little clean up and checking the map in the room then I was off. Other then my stomach gurgling and a little gas, I was ready to hit the road. Maybe one more banjo visit before the road. Well, when I pulled down my pants, I was a little surprised to see a wet spot on the crease. But, not nearly as surprised as the OMG! What have I done!? When I dropped my underwear, I had unloaded a trough in them and had not even noticed. Well... I carefully took of my shoes and pants, then underwear, which went straight into the garbage. A quick shower redressed and with one roll of stolen toilet paper I was heading out of Guerrero Negro. What a day so far.

The road out was dirt, but the highway was new, just one or two years old at the time. Riding or driving in the Baja desert morning and evening is quite spectacular in many ways. The color of the sky, the smell of dew, the magnificent shadows and shades from the light. Just watch out for the toupees. Those are bumps on the highway in and out of town. Usually three to five inches high and three feet wide crossing the road. Hit them at seventy miles/hr and the motorbike front wheel will bounce and the back-wheel kicks, you'll be thrown off the seat and up in the air. ten or twenty miles/hr is a much safer speed to cross them.

Driving this stretch of highway was a real marathon back then, and still is now. Only a few small towns to get gas and many miles of long straight away. Keep your tank full. It is still common for the small-town Baja gas stations to run out of fuel. There is usually a gas station about every 150 or 200 kilometers but don't count on it. Back then it was common for some old guy be sitting on the side of the road with five-gallon jugs for sale at a markup. There was one gas station, more of a kind of a shell of one that I pulled into. It looked like a half build Pemex (Pemex is the Mexican state-owned petroleum company), that had been abandoned. The old guy had one of those glass jugs turned upside down, gravity fed pumps. He put in $5 of gas, I asked where the banjo was, and he smiled and pointed to the side of the building. There was no bathroom just a lot of dried shit and toilet paper on the ground. Well, I did my business anyway and was on my way.

George Jobb

"Adios Guerrero Negro."

CHAPTER 4: A TOWN NAMED MULEGE

Mulege is on the East coast of the Baja and was considered a nice stop even back then. As opposed to Santa Rosalia, the old mining town an hour before. Some say Santa Rosalia has a scenic downtown and is historical to the Baja development. I've worked in mining towns all over Canada, they are what they are, without saying anything nasty. I've spent one night there in eight trips through the Baja.

A river runs through Mulege which looks nice, but you wouldn't want to swim in it. Back in '86 I could only find one hotel. It was run buy a US couple who looked like they were in the witness protection program. Imagine, a beady eyed, dried up old Vegas look. They took my money fourteen dollars which seemed like a lot and showed me the room. Clean with an OK bed. There was a pool too, not bad. Now by this point I was getting a little paranoid about the Mexican water. So, like any normal person I bent down by the pool to take a scoop and smell it. This was noticed by some of the staff who brought it up for discussion. I explained about my diarrhea and developing fear of water. My logic was noted but considered unfounded. I was given extra toilet paper though, how thoughtful.

One of my dreams was to swim in the crystal clear, pristine waters of the Sea of Cortez. So, I set off, I could see it from my hotel window, just a block down the river. However, I should have asked first. The beach was rocky, that's no problem. With my mask and snorkel I waded in. I noticed the water was a little murky. Kind of like English Bay in Vancouver back in the late '60s. Almost sticky, I'm not sure, but it seems to have a bit of an odour. I quickly got out of the water. Standing there, wheels turning, I began to understand. That river was the town's untreated septic field. I was swimming in probably the only polluted section of beach for 1000 miles in the Baja. Fuck!

I showered, took a swim in the hotel pool, then showered again. Well time for some rum, and food. There was a restaurant attached to the hotel. Good place to start. Small, four tables. Patrons included only me and another couple. The guy was in his 40s and let me know he worked in Hollywood right away. His companion was a looker, maybe 25, long legs, tanned, light brown hair. It had been a week without, and in my mid 20s I was still a horn dog. Let alone the eight hours of bouncing my balls on a sport bike seat. Least to say, I was a bit chatty. The old guy had ordered and was slopping down raw oysters, discussing the, "lost art of conversation". Ya he was a crafty old dog. Well, unlike the songs, movies, or rum diaries, no girl leaves sugar Daddy for one night with young stud. Selling your soul has a high price. I've bought a few cheap ones over the years. Another dry night in Mexico. Heading to La Paz tomorrow. Oh boy.

CHAPTER 5: LA PAZ

Heading south from Mulege is one of the greatest sections of the transpeninsular highway. On your left is Conception Bay. Both aesthetically and spiritually it is something astounding to see and experience.

The highway wines like an old river along the coastline. The color of bluish green bays will haunt you forever. Eight trips through the Baja and I have never stopped. The natural beauty is so amazing, like a siren it will seduce you, lure you towards the water's edge. I'm not sure I could ever leave, if I did stop. It would trap me, lull me, diminish all senses, distort my perception of time, lost in a loop. Staying could easily take most people down the dark endless path. Like the bartender owner of Havana's in San Jose who lost seven years in an all-inclusive loop. He ran a bar on the beach in Mazatlán at happy hour. He would talk about the loop. Seven days a week for years running the show for happy hour clients. Fifteen years later, he still couldn't shut it off. Drugs and alcohol couldn't shut it off. You could see it in his eyes. I've pulled myself out of the loop many times. Sometimes excessive partying and liquor or bad relationships. Shitty jobs or shittier employers, at times I was just fed up with the people I was working with. When your ready to break an arm or neck, it's probably a good time to move on. There wasn't conflict resolution thirty-five years ago. No, there wasn't any of that, that's a new thing.

I'm getting older, maybe I'll stop in one of those bays this time, just a few days. What could it hurt?

I filled up and ate some tacos in what I think now is Loreto?

 Not much happening there back in '86. But I did meet an Englishman with his VW bus filled with what I would call junk. But you know the English, it was all treasure. We were about the same age and he seemed to want to give me advice on all. Maybe you've met him. By chance, he was heading to La Paz and knew a good hotel for cheap. It was agreed we would head to La Paz together, about another 200 miles. It was mid-day, no problem.

CHAPTER 6: THE ENGLISHMAN

The Englishman had managed to find the hotel. There was only one road into town, it was an easy drive. The hotel was a little further out of town then I had wanted. It had about forty rooms, single level and completely deserted. The counter guy was small, thin and had that certain kind of look. You know, like he was drunk, stoned, or perhaps had been subject to a lobotomy. Dead eyed. Like nothing was going on in there. I've met a few of these types over the years. Quite often they don't even speak. Personally. I didn't like them then, I don't like them now, and I won't in the future. Sure, as hell not staying here. Next.

Well next was a family run hotel, about fourteen rooms. Looked okay, $2.25 a night. I checked in. Looking and being are not always the same in Mexico. After a meal and some beers, I was back at the hotel, tired and ready for bed. I let myself into the room, to find the old drunk manager of the hotel is sleeping in my bed. How is that possible... All of the other rooms are empty. I woke him up and pointed to the door. He mumbled something and staggered out. I was too tired to give a shit. I fell asleep and forgot about it.

When your traveling by motorcycle you need to keep on things. Like the oil leak on the left side engine cover. It was starting to stain my shoe. So, there I was, driving around town, looking for something that could be a hardware store. I found one. The manager helped me find the silicon. In English and Spanish, the pronunciations are quite similar. He also supplied a rag and gave some suggestions on applying it. Dried in an hour. It worked so well that I left it on for two more years before getting around to replacing the gasket.

It was still early, and I thought I would try to find the beach. After two hours of looking and just about getting shot by some bobble-head military guy, at a gated road whom I tried to ask for directions, I gave up.

The next few hours were spent washing my runners. Also, underwear and shirts. Jeans looked ok. I've noticed that cleaning and organizing things has a calming effect on me.

Time to meet the Englishman for beers, rum, and food. We were chatting away about our day's events. I mentioned the military guy at the gated road. He advised not to drive or walk up to military gates, by accident or on purpose. I asked if he knew where the beach was? With a perfectly straight face he asked why I would want to know. I was thinking at this point he had spent so much time in Mexico that he had developed the native attitude. The sun had set a few hours earlier and I was becoming a little edgy. Probably due to the Mariachi band that wouldn't leave us alone. I tried to pay them to leave. I think they mistook my intention. If you haven't had the pleasure of hearing a Mariachi band, it's like a kid kicking the back of your seat on a long bus ride, or water running down your neck on a rainy day, or a cat in heat in the middle of the night.

Englishman was even starting to look a little frayed. It was his idea to take me to a real old time Mexican bar. I had thought that that's where we were. On account of the sawdust on the floor and the urinal holes built into the bar at each seat so you only had to stand up to take a piss. But no, after a ten-minute walk, going through an empty lot, then a burnt-out building, we entered a back alley. There was a doorway to a building with two military guys with rifles standing at it and a few other people standing around. We went in and holy shit! There were at least 200 of the drunkest Mexicans I had ever seen. Any nationality for that matter. No one seemed to notice the only two gringos in the place. Looked okay to me, so far. We found a table and I went to the bar to pick up the beers. I got one extra beer for the guy staring at me leaning up against the bar. He seemed very drunk but friendly. It doesn't hurt to be nice in a strange land. Englishman was putting on the grey man act, blending right in, using me as a distraction. Good time to take a piss.

Well I tell ya, it a was a piss I'll never forget. I walked into the banjo. There's a guy pissing in the toilet, another in the urinal, that's normal. Then I see a guy pissing in the sink and still two more into the garbage bucket. It was a small bathroom. Hmm...the urinal had room for two. So, I joined the guy there. As I would find out, there was a good reason that nobody was pissing with him. I was a bit drunk and hadn't really noticed. In my 20s I was a bit nervous while pissing in the same room with other people. Sometimes it just wouldn't run. I was thinking about this when I checked the guy out beside me. Fuck he had his pants and his underwear down around his ankles. Not a good omen. His shirt was undone, but it gets worse. At this point I was too nervous to relieve myself. He started talking to me in Spanish.

He was kind of yelling at this point but not aggressively. He began pointing to his bare sweaty chest. Hmm, it doesn't hurt to take a minute and think during moments like this. Slow things down a bit. He pulls a knife out of nowhere and used it to point to the thick scars on his chest. He was telling a story to me. A life and death story from which he had survived. He had six to eight scars on his chest to prove it. His knife was about eight-inch-long and thin, meant to go between the ribs. He had fought, won and taken it from the owner.

He was a policeman with the La Paz police department. He showed me his badge. He was El hombre, "the man". I think I got him a beer, not sure. I still hadn't peed yet. How could I?

Well, I got back to the table and Englishman was just sitting, staring at his beer. We finished our drinks and agreed it was time to leave. All seemed good. Then some mother fucker, stocky Mexican with silver teeth started bitching us out at the door. The army guys didn't seem to notice. This could have gone two ways. Most people don't like assholes but fear them. I was wondering which way this was going to go when El hombre shows up. His pants on, except I'm his amigo now. We are old friends. Time to get the fuck out of there. Silver teeth guy frowning.

Well that was more than enough for one night. I get back to the hotel, let myself in and there's a three-foot puddle of murky yellow piss in the middle of the floor and a fresh shit in the toilet. No toilet paper and none in the basket. What the fuck. I went to the office, woke them up and show them the shit. They move me to the next room. Great. I fall asleep drunk and tired. I wake up a few hours later, feeling sure I'm being bit by mosquitos. I checked out the room, drank some water, couldn't see anything, so went back to bed. An hour later, now I'm sure I'm getting bit by something. What the fuck, another inspection with no results. At that time, I had never heard of bed bugs. I moved on top of the covers and slept. No problem.

I moved to the best hotel in town the next day. Fifteen dollars a night, no regrets. I would mention the name if I could remember, but I can't. I do recall there being a bar on the first floor with urinal holes build into the bar itself, so you didn't have to get up to take a piss. There was sawdust on the floor, and it smelt of pine, seriously, real nice.

The Englishman wanted to make up for the night before. He suggested we check out the whore house. Well okay, I said. The establishment had one not bad looking woman and a bartender and oh ya, an American girl in her 20s, a little on the rough side, average looking, but he asked her to join us at our table anyway. He explained that the bottle of champagne, which I bought included the Mexican woman, who was not bad looking. I think the bottle was Baby Duck, which brought back memories of when I was sixteen. What the fuck.

After a few hours of drinking and laughing I was ready to go. Now, having a woman on your arm that was already paid for and another giving you the cow eyes may seem like a dream come true, but at 26 the thought of throwing a fuck in to either one didn't interest me. At that age I was too proud to fuck an average whore. A few more rums probably would have lowered my morals, but I was in Mexico and I needed to be sober enough to find my way back to the hotel.

CHAPTER 7: FERRY IN

Englishman knew exactly where the La Paz ferry terminal was. This was the passage to Mazatlán, and I would follow him in the morning. Okay, I had to arrive at nine am. The ferry didn't leave till five pm. That seemed like a long time to load a ferry. In British Columbia, a ferry of the same size will take twenty-five minutes to load. I was at the ticket window. It took forty-five minutes to buy and pay for the ticket. I told the woman that it was for one person and the motorcycle, also that I would like a room. She wrote it down and then set it in a box on another man's desk. I was the only person in line at the time. Ten minutes later, he picked up her note, examined it very careful, then stamped it. He then set it back into the box on the woman's desk. Ten minutes later, she picked it up, examined it very carefully, then set it back down. This could take awhile... A few minutes went by and I was beginning to lose track of time. Finally, the woman moves, she comes up to the counter and tells me it would be fourteen dollars. I paid and thought it was over.

No, a ticket had to be written up. The stamped paper with the cash was put into another box on the man's desk. Ten or fifteen minutes later he picked it up, examined it again very carefully. He put the money into the safe and stamped the ticket with a different stamp. He then put it back in the box on the woman's desk. There were now two people behind me in line. I was beginning to get worried that I might miss the ferry. Only eight hours left.

The woman slowly picks up this final ticket and examined it for the third time, nodding to herself. There was a short conversation between her and her boss, about three or four minutes. Ticket still in her hand, while sweat was running down my face, she then walked over to the window, smiled, nodded and handed me my ticket. This all took place in an eight by ten room with two desks, a shelf and a old safe.

I moved my motorcycle towards the loading area along with a few cars and commercial vehicles. I was guessing they got their tickets yesterday. Over the next four hours, more cars, trucks, and people showed up, finally followed by the police and the military. I guess there wasn't much else going on in La Paz that day. Trucks with produce were unloaded, then reloaded, cars checked, hell teeth were being checked. My motorcycle was checked twice.

Then the entertainment started, watching them load the ferry. Holy fuck, I had never seen anything like it. Cars and trucks loaded, then unloaded, at least three times. Then the winches came out. Men wrapped them around axles or bumpers, pulling them an extra inch or two sideways. The last to be loaded was my motorcycle. They all looked exhausted. I was exhausted just watching them. Finally, they tied it down and I was up the gangplank.

At the top of the gangplank was the last checkpoint, a policeman. He wanted to see my visa. I got it out and he examined it very carefully. He asked if I was traveling by train I said no by motorcycle. He said that the train symbol was circled. He showed me. I had a look, well honestly the train looks more like a motorcycle than the motorcycle symbol did. I asked if he wanted me to circle the motorcycle. Instead he asked where I got the visa. I said at the travel agent down the street from where I live in Canada. At the travel Agency. They hand them out to travelers. Also, I had an extra, in case I lost it. I asked if I should fill out another. He kind of stared at me for a bit, shook his head and said, "no get on." You could see it in his eyes, he was thinking that the visas into his own country were a lie.

I went to check my room out, looked okay. Dropped my duffel bag and went exploring. Walking around the ferry. There were two levels, besides the car deck. Upper front was a clean, but empty restaurant, very suspicious. Most other people had blankets and gear. They were setting up to sleep on the decks. Mostly locals, truckers, and a few travelers. Who wouldn't make eye contact? Not sure what was with that.

I had a snooze; the boat was moving when I woke. I was hungry. The restaurant was mostly empty still. Just me and what looked like three young cowboys of about the same age. I ordered the fish, rice and beans. It came with salsa, a nice big scoop on top of the fish and I chomped down. Then began a burning sensation in my throat like I had never felt before. I tried to scream, but couldn't, just forced a choking sound. Christ, my water glass was empty. With my eyes watering and my hands around my throat I ran up to the bar. The cowboys were now staring and laughing. The bartender was looking scared. I was trying to say agua. I'm not sure what came out. One of the cowboys was still laughing, but also yelling at the bartender. He gave me some ice water and another beer. The cowboys smiled and in English told me to stay away from the salsa. I nodded, thankful for the advice, but still couldn't talk yet. I finished my dinner with a few more tortillas and the best vanilla sponge cake I had ever had. No wonder it's their national cake.

The cowboys asked how my throat was and if I wanted to join them. Good and sure. One of them had a bottle of Bacardi rum. He insisted that we would see the bat he was pointing out on the label by the time we finished it. I wasn't so sure, there were four of us and only one bottle. We finished the bottle and paid our bills. They asked if I had been downstairs. I wasn't sure what they meant. They said that's where the real party was. They were not kidding. Just like the Titanic. Holy fuck, one hundred of the second drunkest Mexicans I had ever seen. Dancing, singing, jumping on tables. Old men, young mother's, grandma's, fat, skinny, you name it. Mostly ugly, but it looked like a good old Irish time. The cowboys were giving a fat guy some sneers, he was at another table, I wasn't sure what that was about, until later, more drinks. At some point, I asked the two army guys for a photo with them pointing their machine guns at me with my hands up. We were drunk, and maybe they were to. They seemed to think I wanted them to rob me. They started to frown, until cowboys let them know it was for a joke. All smiles now, I lost the photo of them pointing their guns at me, it would have been a great keepsake.

Now I might have been drunk but I clearly remember the washroom. Which I had to visited more than once. There was three inches of water, puke, shit and toilet paper sloshing on the floor, back and forth as can only happen on a rocking ship. Don't fall or slip! It sobers you up right quick. It seemed like a good time to sneak off towards my room, maybe wash my runners.

Up into the top bunk and asleep in minutes. Lights come on a few minutes later and a fat Mexican came into the room. Shit, they double booked the room. He mumbles something and crawls into the lower bunk. I remembered him from the party downstairs. He had been hanging out with some large older women. Off to sleep land again.

Jesus, I'm woken up again... The bastard's reaching up and touching me. What the fuck!? The fat fuck, he can't even get out of his bed without grabbing onto something. I give his hand a swat and tried too fall back to sleep. Well fuck me, I'm woken up again and now he's trying to reach up and play with my cock.

The predator was drunk and thought he would try to have sex with me, uninvited. I raised my head and slowly slipped off the top bunk. I didn't make a sound as I hit the floor. Now I was standing beside his bed. He lurched forward off the bed and continued groping me. I rested my right hand on his shoulder sliding it behind his head, then moving behind him, my hand and forearm drawing the ark. Now gently resting my arm on his upper chest with my hand on his shoulder. I was still no threat, he smiled and leaned back into me. He was excited and his breaths were quick, the tension was building in him.

It was easy to rest my other hand on his shoulder and placing one palm in the other. A basic choke hold. But still no threat. At the same time, I quickly kicked the back of his knees out. He crumpled and I stepped out of his way. The weight of his body helped wedge my forearm between his chest and lower jaw bone tight against his throat. At the same time my shoulder gave a quick lift and push to the lower part of the back of the skull, where it connects to the spine. There was a muffled crunching and snapping sound. Probably the vertebrae bones breaking, then the spinal cord tearing. He clawed at both my arms and tried to try to pull them away. His weak body betrayed him, it wouldn't help. The last few breaths hissed from his lungs. His eyes were swollen and wide open as I lowered him to the floor without a sound.

I was sure to put all his clothes back on which took some time due to his girth. It was three am and the boat was still. I could not hear a sound. A quick look out the cabin door, all was clear. Hall ways were empty and dimly lit by the soft star light. Another twenty feet and I was on the deck looking up and down the railings. I was on the port side in the shade from the moon. I went back to the room, heaved the corpse onto my shoulder and carried him out to the deck. I dropped him over, there was a faint splosh when he landed in the water. Nothing anyone would notice. Back in the room I processed what I had just done. Then packed his bag up with the few things he had, along with his shiny shoes, took the belongings to the deck and dumped them over too. I left his shoes neatly on the deck beside the railing. I returned to the room, made his lower bunk and tidied up. Checking the washroom, it looked as if he had never been there. Hmm... Finally, some sleep. I noticed his black shiny shoes were gone the next morning.

CHAPTER 8: MAZATLÁN

The ferry had arrived. They allowed me to unload my motorcycle first as I was the last one to have been loaded the day before. Mainly because a full eight hours was required to remove the forty or so cars and trucks. It is typically easier to navigate coastal towns because the sea or ocean can always be used as bearing. In Mazatlán, the Pacific Ocean is west, and the town runs north and south. Unless its dark, then things become more difficult. Finding a hotel, well, not so easy. There was no signage in the city at the time, but by then I knew what to look for.

Old buildings, probably one or two stories, usually with a gate which often resemble compounds. I had a map, and someone had scribbled down directions to and circled a hotel. The bike was still running well, and I was on the road. Always a little exciting rolling into a new town. The coastal road was near the ferry terminal. Just hang a left and see where it goes. Traffic wasn't too bad, easy to look around. Old township on the right, ocean on left. Just past the bend in the road, cliff diving and the cheap hotel section can be found.

I headed in and started circling the block. About a half hour later, I found a classic two story with gated courtyard, for parking. The room which I had checked before paying was large, ten-foot ceilings, overhead fan, two double beds, with a shower. No glass in the windows, but bars and shutters for night. A jug of distilled drinking water was supplied each morning. $3.25 a night. All right. As usual, I will do a walk around the neighborhood and to get a feel for the place. There was a bar on the corner, a few restaurants, small stores, and some private or multi family homes. Lots of kids running around, which is typically a good sign. The bus stop and main roads were two blocks away. I had the impression that it was an older family neighborhood.

One of the other guests was an American, retired school teacher Richard. Older and single, living off a small pension, that goes a long way in Mexico. Richard was writing a book, a dictionary. He would make coffee in the morning and invite me over. He was from New York, Richard said he liked the weather and Spanish women. I'm not sure why someone would seriously attempt to publish a dictionary, as there is heavy competition in the market. Some of the other tenants were vendors or traveling sales guys as well as a few old hookers, who tended to hang their rather large underwear from bedroom windows which faced the courtyard. Why? Well, I asked the American teacher and he said that hadn't noticed. I think he needed glasses.

I would take four or five days to explore the city and beaches and I was looking forward to it. I asked a few people at the hotel where the market and town center were. Not to far, just head up to the corner, hang a right and start walking. Within in a few blocks there was noticeably more people as well as shops, tiendas, panaderias, and restaurants. I picked a restaurant on a second floor, with an outside balcony and a good view of the action on the street.

Ok, not getting any service... What's wrong? There seemed to be a counter with food behind it, so I lined up and started pointing. They started yelling at me and pointing. I wasn't sure who was in the wrong here, but I thought this is just how they communicate.

I'm not really a yeller. I consider it rude. I'm ok with pointing, which got me a bunch of food on my plate as they passed it around. Now, to pay. They were yelling again. Myself, I was smiling, nodding, and staring at the food. I think it was about a $1.25, that included a large glass of fresh melon juice. I sat down at an empty outside table by the railing.

Within a minute a guy shows up with an old arc welder, some cables, and what looked like a piece of coat hanger that he was using as an electrode rod. He started welding the railing beside my table, while I was eating. He was about three feet from me. Sparkes started flying which were landing on me and my food. I was half blinded from the ark flash before I could get up and move to another table. It took a few minutes to regain my sight, other than a few black spots that were now floating around in my left eye. It eventually cleared up.

That was a good lunch. I saw another customer with coffee. After a little wrangling, but less yelling I had one too. I think they added cinnamon, also I think they were warming up to me. They probably thought it was funny seeing the gringo with sparks flying at him. Time for some more exploring.

Back in 1986 there was a large indoor market, housed in what might have been an old military building. It was the size of what now is called a big box store, but back then, those hadn't been invented yet. Wonder where they got the idea... it had everything. Live or dead, veggies, fruit, clothes, leather, etc. At first, the smell would almost make you puke. I got used to it, quick. Didn't bother me after ten or fifteen minutes. What it smelled like was real food, fresh, raw, and ripe, unlike the sterilized, green and half ripe stuff you get up North.

However, the meat section was a little funky, but the bread and pastry sections still make me salivate thinking about them. If you get there in the morning by 9 or 10 there are almost always fresh, sometimes even still warm. one of my favorites is there traditional dish flann, it's like a moist cake always tender, vanilla flavored, you can't go wrong with it. You haven't lived until you've had fresh bread and pastries from an old time Mexican panaderia. The bread turns hard as rock within two days so only get what you need and eat it quick. Unless you are planning to make croutons.

A while later I returned to the hotel. I was missing the motorcycle. It sounds odd, but I just liked staring at it. Still do.

I tend to walk up to it and just admire for a while or crouch down and examine its detailed components. Particularly if I haven't seen it in a while. Sometimes I'll even bring a drink for the visit. I live in a Highrise now, in the winter I'll go down and sit with it. Sometimes even start it up and do a short run around the underground parking area. When I had a driveway and garage it was easy to bring a lawn chair. Or maybe just a quick peak before bed.

It has taken years to understand why. I would ask myself the question of, why would I want to go down into a parking garage, or driveway by myself and look at an object. What is my relationship with this machine? Besides functionality or the aesthetics.

I can begin to answer this question with the mechanical aspects of it. It is clear from my choice of occupation that I am naturally intrigued and excited by machines, particularly vehicles. All of its mechanical components are refined and workable. You can touch them, you can see them and hear them when they run. When you sit on it you can drive it, control it, without a person it is nothing. A relationship is formed through the trust in its reliability that you have projected onto it. Trust that the brakes are going to work, that you can stop and start at will. That if you take a hard corner at higher speeds it not going to slide out. You put your life in the hands of it each time you go for a ride. Of course, if it doesn't let you down, and is continually reliable, with time your trust will grow and so will your belief that it could take you places and bring you back safely.

For example, the handlebars. If they slip or come loose at a higher speed, you've got a problem. Even a simple binding up of the bearing in the front wheel could be catastrophic. You would be catapulted off the bike at fifty miles an hour. This is a major aspect of the admiration I have for my motorcycle. Which I see each time I'm looking at it.

Another is the natural beauty produced by the shape and design of functional art. It creates a sense of passion within me. The balance between the front and back and it's intentional simplicity. A hundred years of designing motorcycles has made them more streamline and life-like, mimicking that of natures fastest creatures. Constant refinement by man regarding their design has maximized these machines efficiency by removing some of the parts that weighed excessively or did not benefit the handling, braking, speed and reliability.

In my opinion, motorcycles are something that you could easily place up on a wall. Just as you would a painting or a sculpture on the mantelpiece. Of course, not all of them, as with all things designed by men there are vast differences in quality.

I know, it sounds strange to some, but I would enjoy seeing half a fuel tank or engine case on display in a home. Even a couple of pistons can rival marble sculptures. Although the wife would probably disagree.

It can't be just me who sees this. I've noticed many t-shirts and posters of engine cases, pistons, and rims. No doubt you'll find them for sale at every car or motorcycle show. Even components seeming basic, like fairings, or a good-looking seat have their own aesthetic quality. I often find myself sitting on my arse, staring at various seats in books or on the internet. I admit it's an odd interest, but I like the various textures, colours, and fit.

And then there are the tires. All shapes sizes designed for particular conditions. Consider a slick street tire, grooved for cutting the rain or a big knobby designed for sand and loose dirt. Tires are objects that you can look at and instinctively know what sort of terrain you'd use them on, whether it's sawdust, coarse gravel, paved asphalt and everything in between.

I don't know what it is, but from all elevations and angles: standing, crouching, from the left, right, or in front there is an elegance. Similar to when one finds a quality sword collection, a saddle or leather works. When something functional has had a great design built into it, it transcends that of just the object's purpose. It sets itself apart from just being a tool. At periods of time in history there have been people that take plain, common objects and create something else entirely. Something with a shape and feel that stimulates your imagination and transcends the realm of material objects. For me, the kings of this realm are motorcycles that were built for travel.

They have unlimited potential. So far, they can take you, how far you can go. Those dreams you had as a kid, to travel and see different parts of the world. To experience a fully lived life. This motorcycle, just sitting in your basement, or garage, or parked under a tarp beside all the other shit in the backyard. All you must do is get on it and let it take you to down those less traveled roads. It stirs emotion and it stirs dreams.

However, this path is not suitable for everyone. There is always that element of risk and danger. It will test your mental fortitude, your strength, reflexes, and your endurance. Not only this, but your will itself. Will you be able to get back on and continue your journey after screwing up or taking a spill, or after you've had a near miss or something more serious.

Thousands of micro movements and decisions must be made continually while riding in an unfamiliar area, broken ground, or heavy traffic. It forces you to focus, to harness the ability of fast paced critical thinking, without hesitation. To remain solidified within that particular moment in time.

That's what I see every time I look at a motorcycle. It's the potential, the unrealized, the unattempted. Potential can easily push you towards the edges of your physical, financial, and mental ability. This object the motorcycle can provide an answer to how far one may take themselves, and whether or not they will even try.

CHAPTER 9: EL CID

Well, I had the neighborhood scoped out and already found a few good restaurants. I walked the block a few times, watching for landmarks and I had decided on a hotel. Maybe even a little partying tonight. I felt it was about time to check out the beaches and the El Cid.

My uncle used to tell me that it was the best hotel in Mazatlán. He had made money in the mining industry and had spent winters there in the '60s and '70s. I hopped on the bike. The El Cid was north from where I was, along the road by the ocean. Past a few different restaurants and hotels. The road was newly paved and in good shape, which is always an oddity in Mexico. As I approached the El Cid, I saw the turquoise sea on my left, the classic Mexican bleached white and beige building on my right. Senor Frogs is also a well-known party place, it would be difficult to miss. Painted bright green with seating capacity for at least 300. Located just a few blocked down the street from El Cid.

On my first pass, I did not stop, but continued further because I wanted to check things out. I continued forward a few more blocks, may be a mile, then turned around and came back. I pulled into the parking lot and found what I thought was a parking spot. This spot was a curved drop off area made from inlaid bricks and there weren't any lines. I shut the bike off, walked over to the bellhop and asked if it was alright if I parked there. He didn't answer immediately, and we stared at each other for a few moments. I was probably one of only a few tourists who had arrived by motorcycle or even driven, and I had become somewhat of an oddity. He eventually nodded and said that it was okay.

I carried on and walked into the famous hotel. It was a big place with a large open lobby. No one really seemed to be bothered or even notice me. Back then, a gringo tourist could pretty well walk into any hotel down there. No one would give them a second look. I headed out to check out the pool area. They had a few signs for specials, the one that interested me was the morning buffet. It was from 8am to about 11:30 am, looked like a pretty good spread for $3.25. That was the same price that I was paying per night for the hotel I was in down the street.

There were three pools and good beach access. Clean, slow sloping beach, good for body surfing or boogie boarding. There was also a swim up bar which I had heard of, but never seen. The seats are submerged about a foot or so below water and you can swim up and have a drink without ever leaving the pool. I asked a hotel employee if it was fine if I came in for breakfast and hung out, although I wasn't currently staying at the hotel. The employee spoke pretty good English and said it was fine as long I ordered a few drinks and didn't get too drunk or cause any problems.

Well, I was sold, my uncle was right, this place was rocking. I had my spot. It was late March at the time, might have been spring break or early summer vacation. To my delight, there was a lot of young women around, gringos, Mexicans, and they all looked pretty fine. Looked like they were in for a good time, and so was I. I decided that I would come back first thing tomorrow morning. Oh ya.

It was starting to get dark by the time I got back to my hotel, about seven o'clock. The night doorman was on. The new guy gave me the impression that I was imposing on him. He needed to open the gate so I could bring my bike inside. He was a bit chubby. He looked like he had what you would now call, "a sense of entitlement."

It's true though, I was obviously imposing on him, he had

a small twelve-inch television on. I assume that's what he did all night, watch TV, and I was disturbing him. Any ways, I learned later that he didn't like gringos much and that he was an ex-policeman. Got fired from the police force a few years back for extorting drunk tourists. He probably should have found some work doing something unrelated to the tourism industry. I'm not sympathetic towards that bullshit.

All was well. Except I had forgotten to close the shutters and I was on the second floor, with no glass. The neighborhood kids would roam around looking for any open windows to throw watermelon peels into as a form of entertainment. If they notice any shutters open, they'd play a game, how many of them they could throw between the shutters and into the room. I guess they thought it was funny. If I were ten years old, I would too.

I did the same shit when I was a kid. We used to collect dozens, even hundreds of snails in my backyard and catapult them around the neighborhood with a tennis racket or terrorize construction sites. We would shit on construction worker equipment and seats, laughing so hard tears would run down our faces as we did it. Just plain funny at ten years of age. A form of entertainment. Didn't care who it affected. Good old fashion fun.

I guess karma has its ways, because when I opened the door, I found a bunch of melon peels on the floor and hundreds of ants along with a few large cockroaches. All of them chomping down on that fresh melon. I looked out the window, but those kids were long gone. Any ways, I swept up, wiped down the mess and threw it in the garbage, might have flushed it down the toilet. I reminded myself to always close the shutters, then off to sleep.

I woke up sometime later, it was one or two o'clock in the morning. I could hear some muffled yelling, on account of the shutters being closed. I didn't want any more melons on the floor. I open the shutters and had a peak out. There're two guys yelling at each other down the road, outside the bar. They pulled out knives and started fucking swinging at each other. It was dark, but in the dim light I could see that one of them was cut. There was a little more yelling and posturing. Eventually one guy walked away and the other guy holding his arm left too. No permanent injury. It's wise not to be hanging around bars too late at night when all the girls have already left, nothing good is going to happen. Keep that in mind if you're traveling on the road or in a foreign country. Situations like that can easily get out of hand. The drunk man's quarrel will never be worth serious injury or death.

The next morning, I woke up a little excited. I did a light workout, just different sets of push ups and core work, some stretching and then a quick shower. I cleaned up and started packing for the day's exploits. I brought a bathing suit, some spare shirts, sunglasses, cap, and I was off to El Cid.

I parked again near buddy with the blank look, but now he was nodding and smiling. We were friends, similar to some of the bar guys around the pool, they would recognize me and nod or smile. I was probably living one of their dreams at the time, hanging around the El Cid with enough money to buy drinks and breakfast. Those were good times. Might have been the best breakfast I had ever had in my life. At twenty-six years of age, I could eat and eat, and I spent a lot of time eating. $3.25, didn't even have to leave a tip. Fresh squeezed orange and melon juice, organic eggs benedict with smoked salmon, shrimp, all kinds of sausages, prepared any way you wanted. There was also some traditional Mexican fare, it looked and tasted fantastic, but not sure what it was called. By the time I was finished my stomach was so tight that I could barely breathe. I changed into my bathing suit and strutted off to the pool area.

Now I thought the smorgasbord buffet was damn good. But holy fuck, it was nothing compared to the pool areas at the El Cid in 1986. I'm not sure why, but there were A LOT of women. The ratio of women to men was at least five to one. There were groups of women ranged from in numbers from four to eight to ten, spread about three different pool areas, and they were looking good. Now, I don't want to sound like I'm boasting but at twenty-six, I was a 180 lbs. Six foot two, with thirty-inch waist and seventeen and half inch neck. I had already done about eight years of judo, one-year amateur boxing, and four years of karate. When I worked, it was twelve-hour shifts, seven days a week, for months at a time. Diamond drilling, it's a very physical job and tough work, the kind that thins out the herd, really quick. In the off season I would do martial arts, hit the gym, hike, bike and river kayak. I was the dude living in Kitsilano at the time, so needless to say. I was looking pretty good, lean and fit.

On one of the nights I had set something up and was going to meet someone at a restaurant bar. The bar was the infamous Senor Frogs. It was somewhat famous at the time, it had t-shirts and similar bars were set up in Acapulco and Puerto Vallarta. Definitely one of the more recognized bars known by Canadians and attracted a lot of tourists who were all looking for the same thing.

I got there around seven or seven-thirty pm and it was already starting to get a little lively. I hadn't had anything to drink yet so I started slow, with a few Pacificos. It was hectic place, but not dangerous or too crazy. About four or five Pacificos later and I found myself sitting with a group of Gringos. It was decided that we would order margaritas.

We were all still what I would consider sober at the time. Hell, what's the harm, they tasted pretty good. I guess they had used brand name tequila. I'm not sure what else was in there; ice and lime maybe. They were large, the size of a soup bowl. Had to use two hands to drink the damn thing. It took an hour to slurp that down and we were all getting a little tipsy. The bartender must have noticed this. It was getting later in the night and naturally we ordered another round. Well, I think they might have spiked the next one or used some of the cheapest, raunchiest, shit tequila on god's green earth. The type of stuff that can make you blind. I'd had at least six or seven drinks at this point over some four hours. It tasted a little different, but you know, it still went down.

Within about half an hour thing were becoming fuzzy. You know, like when you start to get tunnel vision from standing up to fast or getting choked out. I recall people had gotten up on tables by this point and were writing their names on the rafters and ceiling with lipstick. This was also going on at two or three other tables.

The waiter was one of those stocky guys, probably used to moving a wheel barrel around and had been promoted to working the bar. He was as thick as a post, both physically and mentally. Well, he started trying force people off the tables like an imbecile. He was dragging the chairs and tables out from underneath them. He'd be thrown in jail and the business would have their asses sued off anywhere else in the world for doing that shit.

Anyways, he had some trouble with myself and the guy behind me. We were jumping around and taunting him. We ended up getting down. I was told to leave. Oh shit, I was fucked up by this point. I could barely walk or think for that matter. I had to get on my bike and back to the hotel, which somehow, I managed to do. The door man let me in. I think he was just as drunk as I was. I get in my room and instantly I started puking.

I tell ya, that first puke came out like a fire hydrant. It was a disgusting mixture of taco salad, cheap burritos and a gallon of alcohol. I don't know what they put in that last drink, but I was shitting and puking for probably four hours. Now, if you haven't had that experience of alcohol poisoning off cheap Mexican liquor before, it's great. Let me tell you. The beginning is a cakewalk, that's when you still have some foreign liquid in your stomach. When that runs out, you're in for the real fun. You'll puke up a bitter green brown muck called bile. It's a mixture of broken-down red blood cells with digestive enzymes from the pancreas and liver. It burns your throat and the abdominal muscles hurt like hell. You'll be shitting your brains out at the same time. Your ass will feel like a jalapeno. By this point you are sitting on the shitter, hunched over and likely naked, shitting and puking in the same shit paper bucket, that's where you put the toilet paper in old time Mexico. The smell of it all adds to more puking. I had water in the room which I managed to keep down until I was able to past out. I think I lost the next day.

Moral of the story, don't drink margaritas in Mexico unless you make them yourself or you watch them pour the good stuff, although they might have just refilled the bottle with something else. If you're drinking in a bar, sooner or later they will swap the tequila out with the cheapest shit they have. In '86 the cheap shit was $1.25 a gallon for over proof tequila. I had taken a whiff of a bottle, when in one of the stores by my hotel. It smelt like turpentine. You can likely use it for cleaning and it's the same price. Remember, beware of the "margaritas."

Of course, not all nights were like that. Most young men might think that spending the night with two women is a real fantasy. Maybe even some older men. The reality is it's not like the movies or Harlequin novels, you've hardly arrived at the gates of heaven my friend. It's something else.

For example, you've got one girl jumping up and down on you. You're on your back. Because there's two of them, it's going to be harder to keep that timing, if something pops out when she's coming down hard you could get injured. If it just flops to the side no problem, but there's always that possibility. So, you've got to pay attention to that. Now, turn your attention to the other one. She's riding your chin to your nose like it's a skateboard. If she's trimmed really short down there, it's like sandpaper after a while, and she's not going to give a fuck about your sensitive skin. But hey, you signed up for this. There's no changing your mind now.

You knew what you were getting into. There's no bullshit here. It all sounds nice, and then… you orgasm.

The one on the lower side of you doesn't have much to work with now, but she signed up too, she gets down there and starts chomping on it, wet, dripping, and still warm, but she's no quitter, no sir. Now the other one is too flushed to know what's going on and by now she's been riding the skateboard for a while. So, it's like running down your face, but at least it's warm, moist, and without much odor, not too sticky either. Then they switch like a tag team WWE wrestler.

Don't worry sailor, keep in mind you're probably young and in the prime of your life. So, now they've switched and the other one jumps on that. Nope, she doesn't clean anything up, she doesn't give it a wipe, not a wash, nothing, she just jumps on there. This is your dream, your fantasy, you're fulfilling it. At this point the other ones hopping up and down because she's ready. She started slow, because you're not quite 100% yet. But the one sitting on your face is thinking, why take the time to wash up? I've got a rug cleaner right here.

So now she's back at it, going from your nose to the bottom of your chin, back and forth. Sometimes she's pressing down. Other times its light, she might even stop for a bit. You're in control again. At this point, stuff is running down your face, and your chin. It is getting caught up in your nose, it's thick, jam-like because there's a mixture in there. But you've done good work so far and at this point she is flushed. Not just her eyes are dilated, I'll tell ya.

At some point you'll come a second time. The little guy is going down for the count. He's going to need a break. The two girls have had a good time and they're ok with that. Now at this moment you don't want to appear to be in a hurry, you've got to slow things down. You suggest that you've worked up a bit of a sweat, to put it lightly. Don't tell them they have semen dripping down their face, in their hair, all over the bed. Not just yours, but also what's dripping out of them. So, you suggest a shower, politely.

It's nice, you get cleaned up, some soap, warm water. You should wash up top and down below. Everything is nice and clean and you're a gentleman again. You're back in bed and cuddling. This wasn't just about sex. Now you've got one on each arm, it's nice. Usually you have all been drinking, so you are now ready for a snooze. I don't know how many of you had a woman fall asleep in your arms, it's all nice for an hour or so. But then you wake up your arm circulation is cut off and you can't really roll over. You're pinned down, it's impossible to sleep like that.

A tactic I've developed in this situation is to start snoring, even if you have to pretend. I do normally and don't need to practice. The odd time you might get punched in the head. That's an acceptable risk. That's your play, eventually start snoring loud enough that it eventually gets them to move to another bed or couch, maybe even leave. With that you can get a decent night sleep.

That's the low down on spending the night with two women. Pass it on. Basically, to be able to juggle that shit you'll need to be a man. Kind of like going to a bar and taking home the women with the largest breasts. She's confident, and you'll have to be also.

More advice, in tropical climates, Mazatlán as an example, you need to look after things. Remember if you are not sure what's going on down there, stop in at the pharmacy. The pharmacists are usually well educated and can help you out. Learn from another's mistakes. I never noticed until my last day in Mazatlán that my cock was looking a little shriveled and reddish. Also, a little rash was starting between my nuts and leg, I was somewhat concerned. I thought I would ask the retired teacher Richard in the room next door for an opinion. He usually had one. He thought it was a heat rash, quite common. Nothing to worry about, recommendation is to rub some Polysporin cream on it for a few days. Thank goodness, after a few days it was looking as fit as a fiddle. I don't tell many people about that. It wasn't the first time I picked up a little friend down there. When my boys were quite young and I was reading bedtime stories, at the end I'd say, "don't jump out of a plane without a parachute." Maybe I should have taken my own advice when I was younger.

At times like these, you'd best get into a routine. This was mine; I'd wake up, clean up then get my ass down to the El Cid. Then eat and start moving around to a few spots by the pools and check out what's around. After that I usually hit the beach for some boogie boarding or body surfing. Come back into the El Cid, dry off, and size the crowd up. By two or three o'clock you kind of want to make your move. So, you can set up a dinner or a meet time in the club. You've probably had enough sun by then any ways. Before the date, I would usually head back to my hotel. Still found it funny that a meal at El Cid was the same price as a night in my hotel. I would clean up, shower and take a snooze. Then head back out for the rendezvous. There were quite a few places around there to eat or party. Night clubs, Senor Frogs and a few places on the beach, it was all good. Most of the time we would end up back at their hotel. If they wanted an adventure, sneak past the security and spend the night in their room at the El Cid. The security personnel frowned on that. Sometimes I would have to bribe security, five dollars was the going rate for security personnel to get lost. If you didn't pay, they would just keep knocking on the door bothering you. You know, guests can only stay until ten pm. I was back the next day and it would all start over again.

There's one evening that keeps popping back into my memory years later. I was out and about making my moves at a big place right on the water. There was at least 300 people jammed in there. Some sort of too loud music playing. Off out on the beach I could see a crowd gathering around someone, I had to go and investigate. Stuff like this didn't happen at midnight to one o'clock in the morning, something's up. Probably a fight, so off I headed.

It turned out to be a guy doing a magic act. Blond, curly hair, mid 20's, lean wiry guy. He looked serious. His assistant was a stocky American guy with an anxious look on his face. The magician was going to chain himself up with handcuffs and be put inside a canvas sack. Then, his assistant would drag him out and throw him in waist deep water. Which means he would be about two feet under rough water in the dark with only some dim light from the bars across the beach.

Everybody watching was drunk but concerned. I wasn't sure he had done this before. It looked like a new routine. I moved a bit closer. Even while intoxicated I remember thinking that this was a little high risk. God knows how, but the magician got himself out of the handcuffs, shackles, chains and popped up about a minute later. No worse for the ware. I gave the magician a two-dollar tip, it was impressive.

Fifteen or twenty years later I recognized that guy on TV doing a magic show. I can't remember what his name was, but by that time he was a professional escape artist. He had stuck with it until he made a real name for himself. I pointed it out to my wife, she said not too many guys do that sort of stuff anymore and it probably was him. When I checked out his bio online, it said he had made his start on the beaches in Mazatlán.

Well I'll tell ya, after seven or nine days in the loop I was nothing but cock and bone. Time to get the fuck out of Mazatlán. I was sure to check the bike over before the return journey, it looked good. Some wear starting to show on the sprockets. Ninety-five horse power was a lot back in the '80s and I'm guessing the sand on the roads was taking its toll. I wiped the chain off the best I could and added some oil to it. It didn't take too long to load the hockey bag and get it tied down. Off to the ferry ticket office.

There were a few people milling around but the line went much quicker than in La Paz. I was watching an elderly woman eat her lunch at a bench with some interest. Along with a few locals. It was quite a spectacle. She looked to be about 100 years old and well worn, maybe ninety lbs. I didn't see any of her teeth. She had a colorful dress on which appeared homemade. Both the locals and I could tell she wasn't from around these parts. Perhaps a local mountain range or cave, but that's not what we were staring at. She was stuffing food in her mouth faster than she could pick it up. At the same time, not spilling any on her dress.

I wouldn't see this again until my own mother was in her late seventies to early eighties. For this time span she would also stuff food into her mouth whenever eating. It was embarrassing going out for dinner with her. My dad would just shake his head. There would be food on her hands, food dripping down her chin. She ate like a horse. Thank Christ she slowed down by age eighty-five, eats like a bird now.

CHAPTER 10: FERRY OUT

The return ferry was loaded with its, cars, trucks, and one motorcycle. I think I even saw some roosters or chickens, being held in cages. Reminded me of an old wagon caravan. This time I was shit out of luck, they didn't have any rooms left. Fuck.

Looked like I was in for a night on the deck, figured I'll probably get some mother fucker trying to grab my cock again. Ate dinner, no salsa this time, that saved me a lot of grief and the overactive bowels. As a gringo in a foreign country, good to balance benefits and drawbacks.

The most noticeable drawbacks are that you will typically be overcharged, and perhaps even yelled at during any transaction. I developed the habit of just looking around the room calmly while I was getting chewed out, sort of playing the dumb card. If they continued yelling, I'd point to myself and mouth a surprise, "me?!" As if unaware of the whole situation. If they keep yelling, I'd repeat the process, for confirmation, then I'd make some sort of eye contact and shrug. That's universal for, I didn't do it. If I perform a second shrug, that would be for, "I didn't know. I'm not from around here." I would then usually scoot off onto the crowd.

So, no rooms available, but hey, it doesn't hurt to check. I knew where the rooms were because I had taken the same ferry ten days ago. At eight or nine pm, when things were quiet, I checked the door of room I had slept in on the way over, it was locked. I start checking the other doors, one was unlocked.

I slowly cracked the door and looked inside, empty. Looked like they were doing carpentry work. The berth was there, but no mattress, just plywood. I stretched out and had a good night's sleep, better than a steel deck and less damp.

I was woken up at seven am by some very polite carpenters who apologized. I nodded, grabbed my hockey bag and headed to the restaurant for breakfast. It was closed, oh well, the ferry would be in La Paz in an hour.

The cantina was open downstairs. I tried that instead, there were moms, dads, grandpas, grandmas, kids, and truck drivers. Everyone is excited and happy about eating. I got in line and ordered tortillas, scrambled eggs, ham, and juice for $1.50. By the time I had finished eating, the ferry was docking. My head was clearing up from the week before. I was starting to like this foreign land and the people.

The unloading began, before I knew it, I was on the road again. The warm light breeze on my face felt great. I knew the roads and the layout, it's surprising how much memory you retain of a land, even after only one pass through it. Getting on my way and out of town was easy. I headed North through the desert, back towards Canada on the new number one transpeninsular highway. It was still early in the morning and I wanted to put some miles in.

Thirty minutes later, I was out of La Paz, heading up into the mountains, through winding hills, making good time. No traffic and a newly paved and open road. Forty minutes through the mountains and I was in the central valley with long straight always and no speed limit. Beware these long stretches, if you make a mistake there's no one around to help you.

The highway then and now, has its hazards. On the long straights it is raised two to four feet off the desert floor. The sand

and soil are built up to support the pavement and prevent water pooling or washout. The sides are at a forty-five-degree angle. There was no pull over lanes, you have about a foot between yourself, the centerline and the road edge respectively. Sometimes there are dirt or sand roads running parallel to the highway. They're used for farm tractors, horses, or broken-down vehicles. Because of the steep inclined banks between the desert floor and the road, if you are not paying attention and go too far over the highway edge line, you are quite likely to roll, either in a car or riding a motorcycle. It is good to visualize what you would do if you were to run off the road as it happens.

I met two young guys who rolled and lived. Their cars were totaled but with a seatbelt on they were okay. Judging by the hundreds of grave markers on the side of this highway not everyone is so lucky. Do not allow yourself to get too tired or develop tunnel vision. Do not travel at 100 km/hr for long stretches either. At 80 km/hr you could drive the highway once a week for the rest of your life.

While driving between La Paz and Guerrero Negro you will find a few towns. They are small but likely you'll need to stop at one for gas. Between these towns, exists long stretches of desolate and barren highway. At times it feels and looks like you aren't moving, but look down at the speed gauge and read 80 -100 km/hr.

The same scenery will appear to repeat itself, over and over. Travel for an hour and the mountains on the other side of the valley don't look any closer. The vast expanse, sea-like of cactus, shrubs, rock, and sand, is endless upon the horizon. The air is dry and sucks the vapor from your lips and mouth. The waves of heat, emitting off the road are relentless. However, these stretches are necessary, they are part of the journey. At some point I saw a motorcycle coming towards me in the distance. As it approached, I realized that it was in fact the same motorcycle, as my own, even in colour.

As we passed, we both looked at each other. It was indeed the exact same bike, make model, and color, which was unusual. I had only seen one other in five years. He was wearing the same style of jeans, runners, and a black leather jacket. He wore no gloves. His motorcycle helmet was black, full face with a clear visor. He looked the same height, build, even body position. The same bag strapped to the back of his motorcycle, a blue canvas hockey bag.

This was the moment when I met myself. I thought about stopping and turning around. As I'm sure he did as well. I slowed, turned around and drove back cautiously, and so did he. We flagged to pull over, there was an area that would be safe. We got off our bikes and stood facing one another, sizing each other up. When we took off our helmets, it was as if looking into a mirror, he was I and I was him. We talked for a while. Our names were the same, our parents were the same, our brothers and sisters... same.

We had gone to the same school and had grown up in the same area. There wasn't a breath of air. Completely dead, not another sound around us. No movement anywhere. Just him and I, standing still. This was long before the Mandela effect. Neither of us was sure how this could be. We both talked about our experiences with deja vu. Remembering people, places and circumstances as this as if they had happened years ago and we're now being replayed. We both remember the bathroom mirrors as kids, that when opened would reflect infinite copies of ourselves. I had lost count of the people who had come up to me and carried on conversations as if we had known each other for years. But I could not identify them. He said the same had happened to him along with answering random phone calls from people who knew him that he had never met. Both he and I had only mentioned this to a few people over our lives up to that point. Only to find out that everyone did not experience the same thing. We agreed not to say anything for thirty years. It's been thirty-two.

I thought I would keep my eye out for him on any trips I took in the future. We each got back on our bikes, put our helmets on, nodded, and took off in opposite directions. The air started to move again. A light wind returned, as did the rustling of shrubs and the smell of the desert. I still do not know what I really saw or who I met thirty-two years ago. Hell, if it was even real? One does not actually expect to experience something like that for yourself. But it felt so real. As real as anything else in my life.

CHAPTER 11: THE ROAD

September 2018 - My BMW R1150GS is out of the shop. There is no more tick. Got her running like a Pfaff sewing machine. Humm, Humm. Oh ya. Valves adjusted, carbs synchronized, new plugs, pop the clutch in first gear and the front wheel comes off the ground. Bikes ready, but still needs some Mexican insurance.

I have what I need, British Columbia registration tags for the year, my personal gear, tools looking good. Made sure to remember extra keys, in case I lose them. I zip tied a set to the front of the bike. Don't tell anyone, but it's a common place to put an extra set. Kind of like front door keys, placed under flower pots, rocks, inside the door light, under a gnome in the bushes, inside a magnetic box, the window sill, or behind the mail slot. Shhhh don't tell. If your kids are idiots, it's under the floor mat.

Had a meeting with Chief last night. We went through the maps, talked about distances, hotels, and assured his wife that I wouldn't leave him on the side of the road. Unless you know, he's dead.

He has good or average health for his age. I was at his house a week prior and noticed a bag for prescription pill bottles by his saddle. Just the normal stuff, blood pressure, cholesterol, some for gout, and acid reflux. That might be normal, but I just take Advil, with rum to wash it down. Not sure which is better.

I had a few rums while we talked, he likes beer, and his wife, wine. Our departure day was not set in stone. We both like dry weather. We were fine with a window of three or four days on either side of the actual departure day. He's retired and I had put my notice in about a month and a half ago. I'm getting antsy and want to leave.

By the third or forth rum we began discussing emergencies. If one guy dies, the other would hang around for the police to make a report, contact family and spent the night in the area. If the bike calf's, his trip is over. If a bike calves before northern California, my wife agreed to drive the truck down with a ramp. The guy with the broken bike would cover expenses. The other would be on his way. The wife's made a comment that it sounded a little callus. Well, that's a woman's perspective. If a bike caff there's not much you can do. My wife also wanted to know if I was going to leave a note, if I were to leave while she was at work. I said, a text or email would be easier. She just stares at me, who knows what's going through her head.

October 2018 - My two side bags are organized, and I've added a small sheep skin to my seat. It was a freebie and it won't pinch my ass like the stock one. The top bag is looking okay. I just need some pesos. I must not be the only one heading South, the currency shop ran out of Paso's, tomorrow at four o'clock they will give me a call. I found a hard case for the laptop too, ya never know when you might take a fall. I'm eager, I'll give Chief a call and leave a message, "How about we leave Friday or Saturday?" Hope he understands. He called back and said his wife wants him around for Sunday, family stuff. Okay we will leave Monday.

I live in a forty-five plus strata building. Lots of retired folk, Germans, Dutch, Swiss and a few of them damn Mennonites. A lot of the fellas, have taken an interest in the old BMW, especially, one who is ninety-four years old, who is in the gym every morning at seven am. He is five foot five, weighs approximately 150 lbs and lively as ever. It was his dream to own and ride a BMW 500CC in the '60s. Unfortunately, he had a family and mortgage and couldn't afford it at the time, "Oh dat vaz a beautiful bike." He says.

A few ask if I'm going to take it down to Mexico in my pick-up truck? I say no, I'm going to drive it down. I usually have to repeat this a few times over the week, then go into more detail, explaining that my luggage would be on the back of the bike. My Swiss neighbour asked if my wife was getting excited. I said yes, but she won't be coming. She's looking forward to the break from me. I'll see her in two months.

"Vat do you mean?" she asks. I tell her that my wife's working and loves her job. "Ha Ha you have a good wife," she says while poking me with her ninety-six-year-old finger. She's five foot two, weighs approximately ninety-six lbs and does four-kilometer walks pushing her four wheeled walker, two or three times a week, depending on weather. Also, an hour and a half of aerobics in the pool every day. She been a widow for twenty years, has children, grandchildren and great grandchildren. I asked her, a year or two ago, why she had not remarried? There's lots of older single guys in the building, I hinted. She said, "she's not babysitting, cooking for, and pushing some old man around in a wheelchair all day, no vay."

Well, I think I know who wore the pants in that family. There is another neighbor, this fella drives an electric wheelchair, so he'll come scooting around kind of aggressively. He uses a small hand control that sits on his lap. On rainy days, he laps around the underground parking area. The story is that he has had four strokes. I'm not sure how the hell he's still alive. Still seems like he's fairly alert too. When I'm in the underground checking the bike or doing an oil change, he'll hang around for twenty minutes. He is a little temperamental, perhaps due the effects of one of the strokes. For example, one time, when another neighbour came through on his way out, this guy in the wheelchair turned on a dime and scooted away. I assumed they don't get along. The neighbor then looks at me like I should ask, I don't.

I don't want to know what their story is. Christ, I'm just trying to get my oil change done. We chatted for a while anyway. Two weeks later, he died in his apartment, heart attack, he was just fifty-four. Ya just never know. He had an older YJ Jeep stored in the underground parkade and a Zodiac with a trailer parked outside, both not running. I wouldn't mind picking those up cheap.

MARCH 1986 - I could not stop thinking about the visit with myself, it plagued my mind as I drove down through the desert valley. Not until there was a change of scenery did my mind wander onto other topics again. It was a welcome change to go through the Peninsular mountain range. (The Peninsular Ranges stretch 900 plus miles from Southern California to the southern tip of the Baja California). The road wines with dips and curves, up and then down into the next valley. On the straight away I would engage the throttle lock and drop my hands to the motorcycle tank. Steering with my head, leaning one way or the other for miles at a time. At higher speeds the bike wants to go straight. Just a little lean of my head to the left or right would move it a foot off its track.

I came upon the old gas station, I had stopped at on the way down. I was low on fuel, gearing down I pulled in. The same old man was sitting there by the pump, looked like he had not moved in two weeks. He recognized me, smiled and nodded, then filled my tank. I paid, he waved off the change as I tried to give him a tip. He was now staring at me, as if, through me, off into the distance. He knew, I had been to the mountain and made it back unscathed. He put his wad of pesos back in his pocket and walked back into the empty building with no doors or windows.

It was another hour before I came to a town where I could get water and food. I still don't know how the hell that old guy survived out there. An old school gas pump, a chair, and a deserted building with no doors or windows. I did not see a car or transportation, no water, just the empty building and his old soul.

I made it to Guerrero Negro in the early evening, that's a long haul for one day. After a good ten or twelve hours on the road, I was spent. There was not much traffic and I had only stopped for food, fuel, and that oddity which I mentioned earlier. I went to the same hotel and without much hoopla, I got my room setup and had a pretty good meal, fish tacos. I must be starting to blend in because no one gave me a second look when I drove through town. I had a good night's sleep.

The next run will be for the US border and Long Beach California. I was up early, had a fine breakfast of huevos rancheros. That's fried eggs on tortillas covered with fried onions and peppers with a spicy red sauce. You know you can order that in Canada or the US, but it just doesn't have the same flavor. It is very difficult to do Mexican food justice, there are some favors which never quite come out right up north.

I got my ass back on the highway, that will now take me to the coast. There was still not much traffic Real easy to pass anything with ninety-five horse power. I probably average eighty miles an hour, except through towns. Only stopping in several of those dust buckets for fuel. Back in '86 the Baja was still deserted until you got close to Ensenada, just scattered small rural farming communities. Not much traffic in the small towns either. I don't recall any traffic lights? Once you get into Ensenada it gets busier, it was considered a party town.

It was around five or six at night and I was getting close. I took the highway along the Pacific Ocean as far as I could, then cut inland up to the border. I was back on the main road through town. By this time, I was a bit of a "ringer", so I had no trouble getting through traffic and finding the border. At the US border, there was not much of a line up. The border patrol officer was checking over my passport and commented that I had made it back in one piece. I do not recall them even checking the motorbike over, just scooted me through into California. The next stop was finding my aunt's place in Long Beach.

After crossing the border, I found a phone booth and gave my aunt a call. She was happy to hear from me. I asked if it was all right if I spent the night? She said sure, she's been waiting for a call. It was an hour and a half to get over to her place. She was waiting and all dressed up, not looking too bad as usual. Well, as good as she did the last time, I saw her dress up anyway. She said she wanted to take me out for dinner. I was on for that, so I showered, cleaned up, and put on some clean clothes.

We went out and had a nice pasta dinner at a local restaurant. I had lasagna and Caesar salad. Both of us had a glass of wine. A few people, as before were checking us out. She flirted in her way and I was hamming it up. The bill was paid, and we headed back to the house. We were having more wine, probably the second bottle. Just sitting on the couch chatting, ya know, things were looking pretty good.

The top she was wearing was kind of low cut. She had quite a rack and a nice fitting bra too. I was enjoying the view. As we were chatting, she got up and poured us more wine. The wine was hitting hard, and I was feeling pretty relaxed. She was sitting beside me and snuggling up a bit. Touching my leg while she was talking. Well, at that age it didn't take too much to get me aroused. I tell ya, so I put my arm around her shoulder, she leaned in a bit and started to snuggle.

At this point her hand is on my thigh as were talking, maybe moving up and down a bit on my inner thigh. Now that really turned me on. It did back then, and it does now. As we're talking, she leans in and kisses me. Her eyes were dilated as I'm sure mine were too. So, hell, I leaned in and kissed her back. She said, "are you okay with this?"

I said, "ya we're both adults." At that point her hand starts working my crotch. That was nice, her hand with the skill of a mature women got my button and fly down in a few seconds flat. Carefully reaching in and pulling out my hard cock without scuffing anything. The rub and tug had started, I'd better start reciprocating.

I'm checking out those ample breasts and were kissing, she leans back and smiles then goes down and starts giving me a blow job, with very good hand movement. Some women just aren't that skilled, but not her. I'm working my pants down, making some room and checking out the boobs. They were large, they were nice, and I liked them. The ass was feeling okay as well. I guessed she had been working out quite a bit, because there was some shape to it. It wasn't the ass of a twenty or twenty-five-year-old, but again, it was not looking too bad and I was not complaining at this point.

She obviously had done this a few times before because she seemed to have a pretty good rhythm. She finished me off, after two days of bouncing around on a motorcycle seat, I tell ya, there was quite an eruption. She was a trooper, there wasn't anything left over, no mess to clean up.

She finished up and said, "why don't we pour some more wine?" My pants are back up and I was very relaxed. She's snuggling up and it's obvious that my Ante had been around a little bit. She had been married for thirty-two years, so she knew about the wait period, you know, recovery time. After about half an hour, she says, "why don't you sleep in my room tonight?" I agree. The lights were dim, I get undressed and hopped into the bed. She's in the bathroom ten minutes or so. The little guy had not come back yet so I wasn't in any hurry. She comes out wearing a black nighty. Nothing else, and it's see through, and I watch as she slides towards me and crawls into bed. She was looking happy and I probably had a grin on my face.

We were cuddling and I'm checking out her breasts. Then

she takes my hand and moves it down, expecting me to work a bit. It's obviously squeaky clean. Although, the light is dim, I know she is smiling at me, waiting for some reciprocation. By chance I happen to like eating clean pussy. So, I get down there between her legs. I'm having a look in the dim light; Evangeline's pussy was all trimmed up. This was 1986 and ya know that was fine by me. Not like back in the '70s when if you went down on a woman, one never knew what to expect, it was usually a fuckin' jungle. She had done a nice job on it, clean as a whistle I tell ya. I put in my dues, front to back, I'm down there with lots of tongue and movement.

A Brazilian buddy of mine once commented that I should eat pussy with the same intent of a starving man licking up a dinner plate. I was not hearing any complaints. Usually, I would have the hands moving up and down on the thigh for awhile. Until they relax a bit. At twenty-six this was my tried and true technique, hasn't changed much since then. Now I am hearing a few little groans and moans. She was definitely enjoying it. I ran one hand under the ass, caressing that and the other hand under the thigh or around to the top of the pubic area. Massaging the fleshy bit just above the vagina. I'm massaging the area and moving the tongue front to back, exploring, getting a rhythm going. Listening for cues. The intensity of the moans and groans is increasing. I had been down there half an hour by this time. Her body is tensing up and releasing again and again, then she seemed to completely relax. I was guessing it had been a while since she had, had an orgasm. I am not embellishing it, but I think she had a few.

I had been checking things out while this was going on and she was feeling pretty tight. Now I know she didn't have kids, but I'm guessing it had been a while since she had straight sex. At this point she grabbed me by the head, and I mean the one on my shoulders, she pulled me up on her and I slipped it in. I was more than ready. She was very tight and wet. I didn't ask how long it had been since she had had sex, but I'm guessing years. No way she had been doing herself either. In my experience, the second time around most women will tap out after twenty minutes or so. There were a few over the years that would keep me up all night. Some would even wake me up after an hour's snooze for a third or fourth round. This was the first time I had been with someone in their fifty's and we went at it for quite a while. It was probably thirty or forty minutes before I orgasmed. I shuddered at the intensity. It was quite something as opposed to, "I think I'm done?" Afterwards, we cuddled a bit and I was off to sleep.

After that experience I always told men, young and old to, "broaden their spectrum" when looking at women or checking them out.

The next morning, she was pretty cool with it. I cleaned up with a shower, she was already at the table with a great breakfast served. I was starving, she was quite impressed with how much I ate. I just had my shorts and T-shirt on, she was dressed casually. Then it was, "Oh, will you help with the dishes?" Ya sure, I don't mind doing dishes.

I am at the sink, washing stuff up, she comes up behind me, reaching around and starts giving me a rub. Wow, I was liking that as I washed plates. Within a few minutes, I'm aroused then my shorts are off. She slips in front, then down on her knees placing her right-hand thumb and index finger around my cock working it at the base, her left hand is now coupling the back of my balls. She worked a slow steady rhythm with her mouth around the big guy. I was now slightly bent over with my hands resting on the counter. It was as good as the first time, on the couch. It was a pretty nice way to say thanks for the evening.

I hung around another night, we ate at home, then it was the same routine and it was just as good. It was interesting. She was mature and didn't mind pleasing herself and me. Anyway, that is my experience with an older woman. I'm not complaining.

I left her house, early on a Sunday morning, by eight am.

She figured that would be the lowest traffic day through Los Angeles. I had a full tank of fuel and a good breakfast. Driving out I took, I think the 405, then connected onto the I5. I made some good time. Those Californian highways are built for speed. She was right, traffic was still light back then, on Sundays. Once you are out of the Los Angeles area it is just flat open valleys and fuel stops. My mind, balls, and cock were in a happy place.

I made it to Sacramento and started a grid pattern at the second or third turn off. I found a hotel in what looked like an upper middle-class neighbourhood. The lots were a little bigger, with grass and palm trees on the boulevards. The hotel looked new, one level, modern and well maintained. I was a bit cheap and the clerk at the front desk wanted eighty-five dollars a night, back in '86 that was twenty to thirty dollars on the high side. I said, "I would like a business rate." She was polite but responded with, "no, no that's the rate." Then she tried to explain to me where I was. I said that that was nice, but in my opinion, it looked like a dust bowl with some irrigation, nothing personal.

Then she rolled her attractive eyes. There is now a line up but I'm still negotiating. I was used to bitching about prices, so no problem here. Now the people behind me have begun rolling their eyes too. Who the fuck is this kid? Why isn't he at the Motel 6? Holy fuck, if I could have found one, I would have been. I was tired, I didn't want to look anymore. The final outcome was that I got a bit off the price because the room had some problems.

"None that I would notice," I was assured. For seventy-four bucks, I had a room. It was a clean place, but the room was tucked away in a corner. I have stayed in better places thirty-five years later for the same money. In the '80s California was booming, they could charge whatever they wanted. The clerk was attractive, tall, with black hair. Hard to tell how old she was, maybe mid to late twenties. The older guy and his wife behind me seemed to think I was pretty funny. I was feeling pretty good and I asked her if she wanted to hook up later as she gave me the key.

She kind of stared at me like no one had ever asked before. Then rolled her eyes and said, "I don't think so." I said I would be back in the room by eight pm if she changed her mind. I thought I saw her crack a smile, but she just looked over my shoulder and asked the couple behind me if they were checking in. Nothing ventured nothing gained. With a shrug, I was on my way.

The room didn't come with breakfast, but it had a big pool. Most hotels hadn't yet invented the breakfast with a room. I got a work out in and a swim before dinner. Back in the room by seven thirty pm for a good night's sleep.

I was showered, cleaned up, and had eaten. I picked up a bottle of rum and some sodas to wind down a bit. Around nine o'clock there's a knock on my door, and who is it? God knows, I can't remember her name. Wait, it was Vanetta, the looker from the front desk. She says hello. I checked the name tag that she was wearing to confirm, Vanetta. So, I said come on in. She said sure and mentioned that she had just finished up at the front desk. It had been a busy day. I said, "I'll make you a drink, take your shoes off and kick up."

I might have had some snacks. It never hurts to have a few snacks around. She had a couple of rums and we talked a bit Her last name was Elkhorn, probably German. Had a degree and danced a bit for a side job. We were feeling each other out. I was wearing shorts and she had loosened her blouse and untucked it. I offered to massage her back. Who doesn't like a back massage? I let her slide between my legs and started working the shiatsu points down her spine. By '86 I had years of judo and a lot of injury management. Shiatsu is a Japanese massaging technique, pressure points both for pain and pleasure. I could easily find the tense muscles or tendons, working the length of them. Within twenty minutes her breathing relaxed and the stress in her body melted away.

I suggested a shower. She smiled and said, "only if you join me." Considering the lump in my shorts, I couldn't get them off fast enough. Who doesn't like having their back washed? For that matter, just having everything soaped up and washed down. She was lean, athletic with a dancer build. Long legs and full breasts, her ass had two dimples above them. Jet black hair and blue eyes that were calm, but radiated intelligence. At this time in my life, with a goddess I tended to ejaculate prematurely, actually in this case, as soon as she soaped it up…

Soaping up is my favorite part. I just like things slippery. Fortunately, I've got stamina for seconds and she wasn't in a hurry. I kneeled down and slid my tongue in, working it like soft toffee. My nose might have been in there too. She had one hand on the shower rod and one leg on the edge of the tub. No complaints up top or down below. I had washed every nook and cranny and it was nicely trimmed. Got to love these California women in the '80s. They were ten years ahead of their time.

Flings are safer with a guy from out of town. No talk, no gossip, no stalkers following you around days later, just some good release of sexual tension. I was down there awhile maybe twenty minutes. That's when she reached down and pulled me up. Sometimes I don't come up. I stay down longer. I always thought that it creates more desire. I should probably ask some time. At twenty-six, after twenty or thirty minutes, I was ready to go again. We dried off and headed for the bed. Took the top spread off, hopped in and I went back to town down there.

I was only down there just a minute before she grabbed my ears and pulled me up. She wasn't taking no for an answer this time. I'm not sure who was doing the humping, but we were both banging away like a couple of rams. Did I mention she was athletic? The bed was shaking and banging against the gypsum wall. Her eyes were as dilated as saucers, I'm sure that wasn't the only thing. I am guessing she hadn't had a decent hump in some time. She slowed down just as I was coming, her whole body tensed up, legs, abdomen, chest, and arms. I wasn't sure what was happening. Then she relaxed. I rolled off and she rolled towards me onto her side. Then just watched me like a cat. I said I needed a quick shower. She smiled and lit a cigarette. You could smoke in the rooms back then.

She was finishing her cigarette by the time I came out. Said something like, "too bad you're just passing through." She got dressed and blew me a kiss on her way out the door. I looked her up some years later, but never contacted her. She had two kids by then and was living with the father, not married. Worked for the school board I think, maybe a counselor.

That night I dreamed I was sleeping on a beach, the steady rhythm and vibrations of the waves flowed through my body, drawing me into a deep sleep. There were people standing around me talking. Discussing something of concern. I could not understand what they were saying. I woke up the next morning feeling rested, but I felt as if something had changed. Something just on the edge of my consciousness, which I couldn't quite pull into focus. I was thinking about Vanetta and the night before but couldn't connect it to the dots between her and my dream. My bags were packed, and I dropped the keys off at the front desk. She wasn't there, just some poker-faced guy.

CHAPTER 12: SACRAMENTO

The bike was running good for seven thousand kilometers and no major issues so far, but I can tell that the chain and sprockets were ready to go. There was noticeable rattling and the chain would skip a link if I gave it too much throttle. Heading out of Sacramento, I still had that woman on my mind. I couldn't shake it even after an hour. She cast some sort of damn spell on me. It was still early in the morning and the air was fresh. I could feel the warmth of the rising sun coming through my leather jacket. Traffic was easy. The commuters faded off onto the turn offs. It was just me, other travelers, and the truckers. I was getting into a groove, listening to the hum of the engine. Ignoring the chain rattle, I'll look after that when I am back at home. After a couple of hours in, I pulled over as usual for food and fuel. I gassed up first and did a quick check over of the bike. Only one basic restaurant in town so I pulled in and sat down. It doesn't hurt to read a menu, but back then it was usually bacon and eggs easy over, brown toast, coffee, and water. There was a sign on the table explaining that it takes three cups of water to wash a single cup. Suggesting you should not have a water with your meal. You don't see those signs any more. I'm not sure what sort of retard came up the those.

So, the waitress gives me a little sigh when I ask for a glass. Write something on a sign and most people will believe it. No one was moving too fast today, or maybe it was just me. It seemed like time had slowed down for everyone around me. Could have been that I was just processing things at a faster pace.

After pilots end a dogfighting drill, it's customary to take a five to ten-minute low speed cool down flight before landing. When the body and brain is pumped full of stress hormones during prolonged high intensity action it becomes extremely difficult to transition quickly into a relatively slow and mundane task. Imagine a race car driver transitioning from a 200 mile an hour race, into being forced into city traffic. It is hard to just shut your mind on and off that quick. But I tell ya, finishing off a big old greasy trucker breakfast did the trick. I was back in that mundane river, floating down at the same pace with everyone else. Snug as a bug. Even the waitress seemed more pleasant. Or I just wasn't seeing the subtleties.

When I got back on the freeway, I had lost my groove. My movements were stiff, and my timing was a little off. It is hard to hold on to that level concentration for extended periods. I was heading into the mountains just out of Northern California. It's a nice banked highway. Trees become an amazing thing to see when you haven't for a long time. Trees, just trees. They have a calming effect on me. Kind of like a good lay. Jesus, there she is again. A few more stops in Oregon for fuel. Back in the '80s the state was full of good people. It's rougher now, I wonder if the lifers, born and raised can see that? Or when you live within indistinct change day by day the adjustments are so small, you cannot notice them until it's too late and you've become just like everyone else. Like thousands of small cuts, year after year, until you've grown accustomed to the pain, without memory of life without that pain.

I saw a hand painted hotel sign on the North side of Portland. I rode for ten or fifteen minutes and ended up in a small town, quaint place, kind of hippy. Off the highway far enough where they wouldn't get much I5 traffic. Scattered about were some older stores and homes which were still well maintained. The hotel was a historic building on top of a few other businesses. Small railings bordered the upper floor. You could open a double window from your room and watch the street action below. Whatever that may be?

I checked in at the front desk. Wow, the girl was dressed in period costume from the 1800's. I wasn't sure perhaps an 1890 prostitute or a can-can dancer? With a glint in her eye, she explained that it was Klondike era this week and that this hotel has been restored but was once a whore house. She had reddish hair and a great rack. There would be events going on throughout the day. Also, tours, I had picked a good time to roll into town.

I cleaned up, then came back down to have beer in the bar. It was attached to the back side of the check in. Hmm, the Klondike woman had two jobs here. There were a few tourists at tables, her and two other barmaids worked as tour guides. I started chatting with her. She was their leader. By my second beer, she suggested I take the five-dollar tour of the old section of the hotel, where the working girls used to live and work. They had apparently restored it to be historical accurate to the former whore house and "it was quite interesting," she said with a smile.

Well. I had been in a few modern whore houses, but none from the 1800's that I recall. It started as a small staircase designed for smaller people. She led me up slowly. The first room was the kitchen. Seating for four and a small wood burning stove, ice box, cutting table, and a few dishes. The next room was maybe eight by ten. It was the sewing room, of course, in those days they made and repaired their own clothes. I thought it was all kind of dingy looking. A little anticlimactic. The next small room was intended for medical checkups, complete with all the tools of the trade. Apparently, abortions were common in those days. Now it was getting little strange, but intriguing. Next, she took me to the bathing room. She explained that with a little extra cash, the bath included a rub down for the gentleman. I said, "who wouldn't like that." She smiled and agreed. Next, to the action rooms/bedrooms. Well, they were plain, but functional. The sheets were cleaned daily. There was a string attached to a doll.

She explained that when the doll was laid onto its side it would also tip the doll connected at the other end of the string downstairs. No double booking here.

The last room was larger and cleaner. Newer blankets and a deer skin lade on top. This room was for the top producing girl. The price was fifteen dollars and then a cigarette was lit, so you had about fifteen minutes to get your business done. I took out fifteen dollars out of my wallet and handed it to her. She smiled a cat smile, took the money and put it in her bra. She then laded the doll down and took off her underwear, all in under ten seconds. My pants were quickly undone, and a condom installed on my rising cock. She pulled me towards her lying back on the bed at the same time. She was wet and amazing. I was finished with lots of cigarette left burning. She removed the condom and wiped me off as fast as it went on. By the time I had my pants done up, her underwear was back on. She smiled and said, "that's the full tour of the old whore house." She then stood the doll backup and led me down another set of stairs which came out at the other end of the bar.

The two other waitresses asked how the tour was with smug looks on their faces. I said, "very professional," and ordered another beer. I asked what her name was. She had gone over to another table. They said "Rosie, Rosie Silver."

That night, I had dinner down the street. Breaded veal, mashed potatoes with gravy and a few veggies. I saw Rosie walking through town with a group of tourists behind her. Talking about the town's history. Pointing out historical buildings and adding in some folklore. I nodded, she nodded back with a knowing smile. I showered and climbed into bed. My mind jumped from thought to thought, running through the last few day's events. The blankets were cool. I had opened the screened window to let in a cool breeze. The noise of the town drifted away. Eight hours later I opened my eyes. I didn't remember closing them. I hadn't moved, the blankets were undisturbed. No dreams

just rest and blackness. My mind was clear, the body felt strong.
I geared up the bike, gave her a pat on the seat for not letting me
down and headed out of town.

CHAPTER 13: THE LAST STRETCH

I got back on the I-5 and continued my run north. It felt like I was in a different world, I recalled the nine to five working jobs, I've had over the years and wondered what I'd be returning to? Eventually the traffic started picking up, commercial travelers, commuters, myself and the Suzuki 1100. The air was still fresh and clean. I enjoyed it as I traveled through the mountains and hills of southern Washington State. Within a few hours, I was going through larger cities with heavier traffic. During the ride, my thoughts consisted of an influx of ideas, both present and past, extending back into the previous days and weeks. I had been on the road a long time now, like clips of a favorite motion picture they had been locked into my memory.

I passed through Seattle easily, which was the largest city before the Washington-British Columbia border. I pressed forward through Skagit County, a rural farming community. Finally, I arrived at the Peace Arch border crossing. I was stopped and asked a few of questions about where I had been and how long I've been out of the country. I am not sure they believed my answers, so they checked over the bike, not much to look at. It must have looked like I had put a few miles on, there weren't too many further questions. Within five minutes, I was sent on my way.

At the time I was living on and off with my parents. Of course, my Mom was pleased that I had not been murdered or simply disappeared while on the road. After a few minutes of reassuring her that I was fine. Dad was like, "look who made it home in one piece," with a smile on his face. I unloaded my gear and put a load of laundry on. Came back, checked over the bike, and made a few calls, reconnecting with old buddies. After my return, it might have been my imagination, but I had the impression that people were looking at me differently. No idea whether they knew I had just traveled alone by motorcycle down though the United States and into Mexico and back without any problems. I recall, on the first day out after arriving home, people seemed to avoid eye contact. Like it somehow made them uncomfortable. It was probably just the set lines in my face from putting in those long hours on a motorcycle, or maybe just the focus in my eyes that was difficult to turn off? Perhaps they just saw something a little different in my eyes?

I returned to training Judo as soon as I got back. My regular training partner at the time was Mike. At that time, he had been training heavily for three to four years on top of a previous twelve years and was now placing competitively at a national level. Mike was one of the few people who commented, he said he felt something was different, something had changed in me. We trained together and fought two or three times a week. He was not specific, it may have been something different within my fighting style? The world was smaller now, at least to me anyways. It was after that trip that I realized someone could drop me anywhere, anywhere in the world and I could get by. I could make my way back or start a new life wherever I was. It fostered a personal sense of strength and self-assurance. Reflecting back on it, I wonder if other people were seeing what Mike felt when we fought? Much like the trip, I just carried on.

I had been watching things, like the texture of the road, or other cars, debris, or dust in the wind more carefully. The minute to minute decisions you must make, all going through your eyes into your brain and back into the body, after hours and hours of being on the road checking your peripheral vision constantly. Performing the side-to-side movement of your head before changing lanes. It sounds easy, you think that it would become quite instinctive, and it does to an extent, but the drawback is hidden within mistakes. Or maybe it's just my imagination. Or perhaps people just do not like to make eye contact.

People who ride motorcycles regularly, or even bicycles tend to be able to hold their focus for longer periods of time. You cannot help it, it is what you need to do every time you go on a long ride. That is why people love riding, why they keep doing it. Even when they are probably too old, or they know their reactions are not as good as they used to be.

Many things, power, money, relationships, strength, or speed are all difficult to give up. Once you have them, you don't want them to slip away, you fight it, like trying to tell elderly parents who have trouble looking after themselves that it's time to move into an old folks' home. Even though it's for their benefit and they would still be among friends and people with similar interests and stories and life experiences, they still fight any change.

You keep fighting and you keep fighting, you may get knocked down and beat up, but you must still get back up, and work at what you want again. Riding, like many things in life, metaphorically represents life itself. Your ability and your willingness to keep trying, to keep struggling for something else, even if you cannot see, feel, smell or touch it. Somewhere inside of you will know that desire is still there, possibly atrophied and unevolved. Maybe you've seen that skill set or attribute before when you were kid, or you saw it in someone else and thought that maybe you could do that also, maybe just maybe if you kept trying and working towards that goal, one day you could achieve it too. Or achieve more, create something new, combine two or three different things that hadn't been combined yet and manifest something unique with your mark on it. Whether it's a year or two years or ten years or a hundred years later. If even only one person was too hold or read or see what you have created and still be inspired. Even to just understand that person's life, or what drove them to push it so far is a means to an end.

CHAPTER 14: 32 YEARS LATER

OCTOBER - 2018. Leaving the Lower Mainland at eight am gets you into Seattle around ten am, missing rush hour traffic. Crossing the US border into Sumas is always an adventure. It is manned by the C team, you know the type. They have gotten the boot from every other US government job and ended up in a border town nowhere. At their best, they are pieces of shit. A favoured game is to drag in elderly people, search their cars for blood pressure and heart medication, then question if they can produce their original doctor's prescription. Telling these elderlies, they could be banned for life from entering the US, for smuggling drugs across the border, continuing until they are almost in tears. But the agents are always smiling as they say it. This is a common game played by both Sumas and Huntington border agents One border agent at Huntington has banned 2,200 Canadians from crossing the border, no reason given. Last, I red, it was before the courts. You may have watched on TV, the border control shows, what they do not show, is the border agents doing cavity searches on the elderly and minors, without any level of suspicion. No reason, other than they can do whatever they want and this they will tell you.

During a shift change, it is quite a spectacle. Usually agents put a cone up, blocking the lane/gate or leave the light red on while two to three of the fat pigs will just stand there for five or ten minutes talking about their day, because they can. They can do whatever they want, just ask them. They will make up fraudulent reports about finding a half smoked Mexican cigar or about some seeds left in your salad, and if they will do that, well they would finger fuck a four-year-old. Because they can do whatever they want. Just ask them. I have met women who have had border agents follow them home. When they asked the pigs what they were doing, they said, "they can do whatever they want."

I have crossed many borders; into Mexico, into Costa Rica, into El Salvador and into Europe. In comparison, I just went through four military checkpoints in the Baja in the last two days. No border agents compare to the pieces of shit at the Sumas and Huntington Border crossings. This is no exaggeration. Talk to anyone who crosses them on a regular basis.

If they were randomly drug tested, they would be fired and banned from working in any Federal position. If they worked for any Police department they would be fired and sued. If they conducted the same behavior in public they would be charged, convicted, and sent to prison and then raped in prison. Then released after three to five years as registered sex offenders because that's who they are. Be wary when you are crossing those two borders.

Well, on this day there were three open gates when Chief and I got there, one Nexis and two regular crossing lanes. It took ten minutes to get across. Ya shift change, LAX manages to process two hundred to three hundred international travelers through twenty-five gates in the same amount of time. That is what an A team can do.

CHAPTER 15: ON THE ROAD AGAIN

Back on the road and hit with hard rains, not real cold, or heavy, but relentless. If you have been in the North West, you will know the type of rain I am talking about. Like a perpetual mist, small droplets. Chief and I managed, getting through Seattle was okay. No major road construction or accidents just normal volume and the rain. We refueled and grabbed a Starbucks. Looks like the rain is lightening up? Nothing like hope on the road. Then it started raining again. Had lunch somewhere past Everett, Washington. Made it to Salem, Oregon (about five hundred and fifty kilometers), for the first night.

I thought Abbotsford had a lot homeless and crack heads. Salem has even more. Picking the cheapest hotel on a Google map search is not always the best idea. Ya get what you pay for. When you are checking into the cheapest hotels, pay attention to the people and surroundings. Buddy, who thought it would be a good idea to go with cheap rather than sleep on the side of the road, picked the motel. While we were checking in, a guy comes in with what looks like a homeless couple and said, "This is the couple I was talking about!"

It's not a good sign. There is a policy in some communities that state something like, if there's no homes or shelters available, a cheap hotel can be provided that will put them up for a night, at the city's expense. I'm okay with this, it's good karma or charity and the hotels comp it at lower rate.

But there is no fucking way, I want to pay for a room at this place. Holy shit, it's majorly fucked up and not in a good way. The partying starts at about six pm, okay, but by eight pm it is getting a little aggressive, lots of people coming and going. Still okay, by nine or ten pm it is a party, and arguments can be heard through two or three layers of walls. Lots of motherfuckers and blow. Get your ass out of there! Then, the cars with shitty exhausts start showing up, followed by yelling, and Police and fire trucks. It is great, if your room is free and it is party night Tuesdays or welfare Wednesdays, but when you are paying for the room and you want some sleep, not so good. The good news around one or two am, it calms down. I am guessing if they do not shut up by one am, they are kicked out. Maybe they should make it six pm…. Hmm.

Hit the road early the next morning, mostly because Motel 6 doesn't have a breakfast. Parking lot is empty, looks like a few people still work for a living. The partiers are still fast asleep. God bless charity types. The work they do just warms my heart. Now, I am sure some of these folks come in handy at election time. These types, kind of blank eyed and sound like they are reading from cue cards. As if not even sure how they got where they are, not dissimilar to Justin Trudeau. The homeless do need help, and training and housing and so on, and dignity. Yes, most of all dignity, because without, who are they? Well, they used to be called hobos. Remember wild and free? Worked when they wanted, hopped the rails to get around. Now, they are the forgotten, the needy, the left behind, or whatever is the news story that day. Will it even make the news or get someone elected? Yes, yes, yes, yes. It is not the government's problem, it is not the state's problem or the city's, it is your problem (common citizens). The people who work or have worked all their lives and are now retired, it is their problem, or they must be the problem, at least they are the causes of it. Yes indeed. Ha ha it is all their problem now.

One of the great things about riding a loaded-up motorcycle across a country is the looks you will get when you are stopped in at the local restaurants or cafes along the highway. I gear down and get ready to order my food. People are watching but pretending not to. It is hard not to notice, people on bike trips always look a little rough. Clothes are a bit dirty, the bikes are a bit dirty, it is hard not to be. In almost any highway restaurant or coffee shop, the morning crowds are usually local who have done a few motorcycle trips in the past. Usually they will watch you for a while, then strike up a conversation with a few questions. Where you from? How far you going? It is nice, it is polite, hard not to like these people.

Your trip brings back memories of their trip. A trucker said hello and that he's been keeping a eye on us. He wanted to know where we were going and if he could come, with a smile. We said sure, and that we were headed to the Baja. He smiled, waved and got back into his rig. We talked to another guy sitting next to us in the diner, dressed like a tradesman, probably a painter or drywaller. He had a pretty good story. He had competed for about fifteen years in off-road motorcycle racing. He had had so many injuries he lost count. He was now married and had kids, so he had backed off for a few years. Then, a buddy talked him into doing a series of ten races. He had some sponsorship and some of the expenses covered because that ain't cheap, there are repairs, travel time, and lost work hours, plus getting injured during the race. It all takes its toll.

I did a lot of competitive sports. Ten competitions in a year is a lot. This isn't beer league baseball or hockey or pick up basketball. You know it is serious when the doctors are on standby, there is an ambulance in the parking lot and people are getting helped or carried off throughout the day. In one of the last races of the season, he took a hard fall and ended up with a broken back for the second time in his life. He was loaded up on a spine board, two or three hours later he was at the hospital, by that time his hands and legs were tingling. That is not good, if you have been around back injuries, but common. He healed up okay, but took some hard advice from all, Doctors, wife, friends etc. He was in his 40's. It is hard to give things up if you are a competitor, but he was older, and the fat lady was singing. He missed it and said, "he wouldn't trade any of it for anything."

I was competing in my sport in my late 30s with one of the toughest partners I have ever worked out with. One day he made an attack and I blocked, he dropped to the ground. He had not ever lain still after a blocked attack, always back up to his feet. He always put out at one hundred percent when he fought. It was a neck injury. Fortunately, we had some smart people in the club at the time. He was stabilized and the ambulance got him to the main spinal unit in Vancouver. They took a piece of bone from his hip and fused it to the fracture in his neck. He recovered and came back to the sport to place at the Senior Nationals. He also now has one badass scar on his neck. What do I have, 3 broken lower right ribs that have fused together? I like to remind him that I am also deformed from when he broke my ribs. It looks like half a lacrosse ball under my skin. He usually shakes his head and reminds me that I broke his fuckin' neck. Yes, but you have a badass scar to show for it and I look deformed. So... how's the wife and kids?

It was the end of day two and we had found another Motel 6. We were obviously masochists. This time we were going to ask a few more questions. The young lady behind the counter was quite nice and polite. Even though we had just asked if they let homeless persons into the hotel? We let her know that we didn't have a problem with that, or charity, but we're not staying here if they do. She said they did allow charity groups to purchase rooms, but if they look sketchy or cause any problems, they are kicked out right away. All good so far. It looked like a better area of town, but not the best. She then sent us to the back side of the hotel adjacent to a public parking lot used by truckers. I think she thought we were the sketchy ones, not sure. The room was quiet, mostly working guys with their trucks coming in. All was quiet by nine or ten pm and we got some sleep. No problems with the bikes or people coming and going.

No breakfast, so we were off early again. We got in an hour or more on the I-5 then started looking for fuel and food. We pulled off the highway and gassed up. There was a McD's beside it, new, big windows, easy to keep an eye on the bikes and gear. We pulled in and ordered our normal sustenance, coffee (dark roast if they have it), egg-sausage McMuffin and hash browns. We sat down, geared off and started munching and talking about the trip and others we had heard of. The fellow at the table behind us starts talking to us, he is by himself, obviously a local, older guy probably in his late 60s. He goes, "ah is that BMW yours?"

So, this guy had owned a BMW K80 from the '70s or '80s and he had put a 150,000 miles on it. That is quite a bit of riding, shit, it was still running well. Original engine and tranny. That goes to show you how well these bikes are built and how solid they are, they can go the distances. The big trip he made when he was younger was getting down through Mexico and into Guatemala, back in the early '80s. He said it was quite an adventure. He had gone with another fellow. I imagine the roads were pretty rustic back then. No cell phones, no GPS, just a map and you were on your way, just see how things go. He said it was the best trip he's ever done in his life, meeting new people, and new experiences. In Mexico or Guatemala, the hotels would have been cheap, the US exchange rate was high compared to the peso back then. He told us if he wasn't so old, he would do it again. He is now looking forward to hitting the 300,000-mile club. He is going to keep his K80 for as long as it keeps running or longer. That was an interesting guy and a great story.

We finished breakfast and got back on the road. We made good miles that day. We drove from Northern California to just north of Los Angeles. Here we encountered rain storms, they so were bad that we had to pull over under several overpasses and wait them out. We put on more rain gear. No fun driving the I-5 in the rain, it was a downpour, droplets bouncing off the road. You could see the rain was pulling up some from crap off the road, which had built up over a long hot summer. It looked like milk, but I am sure it wasn't. We were being sprayed with this stuff, not the best driving conditions. It ended up clearing up like it always does in the big open valleys.

Chief tends to weave in and out of traffic, normally you would only do that a couple of times every thirty minutes, it's no big deal, but when you're traveling by bike with other people and doing it for an hour non-stop, every thirty seconds... it gets a little annoying. I, under no circumstances want to be cutting through traffic, left to right lane, back and forth, every thirty seconds for one or two hours at a time, no way. So, at some point I just hang behind a truck. Driven, by someone who acts like a professional driver. Typically, they are staying between the lines, doing a good consistent speed, five or seven miles an hour over posted limits. I just sit there. They are my blockers and become valuable when you are on a long trip. They clear the road and have better visibility. They are aware of traffic and stay in contact with the other truckers about problems ahead.

So, I will sit there and let Chief scoot ahead, usually he gets a quarter to half a mile ahead. I could keep him in sight when I peaked around the truck or blocker. After awhile, he got the hint and slowed down. Now I don't mind passing vehicles, going below the speed limit. But I prefer to hang with traffic for ten or fifteen minutes before I pass the guy. Then going around and hang behind the next guy. On a 4000-kilometer trip there is not much benefit, it is not a race. You want to be the steady Eddy guy, this is not the Dakar or a European rally. This is traveling by road through heavy traffic and rain on an interstate highway. You have got the commuters in the morning and evenings plus the regular volume throughout the day. Driving in and out for traffic constantly will burn you out. The little extra tension, which chips away at you, wears you down. You begin to feel the constant vibrations and noises, your eyes strain from watching the traffic and there is concern of being side swiped or run off the road.

This is what I have always done on main roads, find a good driver and let him lead for twenty minutes or half an hour, then move on. If you start driving too slowly and it becomes boring, perhaps accelerate before dulling of the senses begins. Most professional drivers don't have a problem with you hanging behind them either. I have done eight rounders from Vancouver to Mexico and a couple of cross Canada trips. No problems so far. I don't like chasing people or being chased. Actually, I don't really like driving on main roads, always felt safer on the back dirt, gravel service or logging roads, no one in front and no one behind.

We made it to just north of Los Angeles by the hump. This night we grabbed a hotel, nice place with clean sheets. Who doesn't like clean sheets after a long ride? This time breakfast came with the room. The food at the restaurant beside the hotel was a crap dinner, but 1 out of 2 ain't too bad. Better than O and O, if you have ever competed. We had put on some kilometers that day, about eight-hundred. That is sure something on a bike. Higher speeds, open valleys, unlimited vision, makes for a high kilometer day. You got to pat yourself on the back once in a while.

How does one prepare for the worst part of the trip? When you are heading down the I-5 the worst part is from north of Los Angeles to San Diego. The traffic is like an endless moving parking lot, if it is not stopped, it is stop and go. When things are moving, traffic flow goes too fast for the volume, then things just slow down again. I find it is more relaxing if traffic flow is stop and go. For this stretch of the I-5, it is probably like that every day. The locals know how it is and just deal with it, as do we all with many things in life. So how do I get through that shit for the next six to ten hours of driving?

Well, want to know how to get through the worst part of the trip? I just think about the great rides. One ride in particular is found outside of San Jose Del Cabo. There is a bridge that heads out of town over the estuary. This goes for ten kilometers then connects to the dirt and sandy ocean roads of the East Cape. Most of year it has a pretty good view. When the estuary is getting ready to flood, it becomes filled by the early fall rains and eventually the sand berm breaks and runs off into the sea of Cortez. It must have been quite the sight a few hundred years ago, image clean fresh water in a desert climate. According to the life long residents there would have been a population of two or three hundred local people plus the odd Pirate living amongst them. It probably looked like an endless fresh water source year-round. The river bed was drilled into recently and found to be at least 800 feet deep. Wells were sunk every ten or twenty kilometers up into the valley and it now supplies water to 100,000 people.

That is pretty good for a small desert town. They receive only four to seven inches of rain a year and it all seeps into the river bed for hundreds of square kilometers. The road along the coast out of San Jose is lightly used and now is mostly paved. Follow that for half an hour and it will take you to a more coastal road, up towards the East Cape. Years ago, you could gain access to the coast from town, but developers have bought up large chunks of ocean front now blocking the road. Those were great roads, good driving. It is still a great route, except you will have to head farther up, out of town. Continue, and head down the beach road, where it is just dirt and banked corners, well grated. For a trail rider, this is a dream. You are riding over undulating hills, through river beds, taking hair pin turns or meandering straight a way. Sometimes it is rutty, especially after it rains, but is usually cleaned up within a week or two. Most of the time, you will likely come across free range horses, cows and donkeys as well as the odd roadrunner or coyote. In October, there are younger colts and steers standing about or on the roadway. You will want to slow down for them. They only stare as you go by. Yup, no one in front and no one behind and the clean, sea air.

Anyways, that is the ride I am thinking about while stuck in traffic, trying not to get side swiped or run off the road.

CHAPTER 16: CHULA VISTA AND THE BORDER

Well, thank Christ we made it through Los Angeles and San Diego. We ended the day at a pretty good hotel in Chula Vista, a Best Western. It had clean fresh sheets and a good restaurant beside it, breakfast included. What we did not know when we arrived was that this particular hotel had acquired a nickname, "the Cancer Hotel." Not because you get cancer staying there, but because of all the Canadians and Americans that come down for cancer treatment in Tijuana that book to stay there and are shuttled by the hotel across the border. I was not aware that this place was as popular as it is. There seems to be an industry growing around it. A few of the older guys around the pool that were close to our age were getting some treatment done for Prostate cancer or skin cancer treatments. The shuttle bus was full the next morning. There can be a long waiting list in Canada, months, even years for some medical treatments. Don't forget to sign up in advance for your hip replacement, its a two year wait in Canada.

We made it to the restaurant by six pm, those we spoke with thought it was funny that we were at the "cancer hotel", but didn't have cancer, and they referred to that fact. Apparently, the locals in the neighbourhood also knew what it was. We still tried to get a discount, didn't work. Everyone was being nice to them, you don't go shitting on people who are dying. Rooms did not get broken into, shit was not being stolen from their cars, if they had one. Even for a career criminal, that would be pretty low, like robbing a person in a wheelchair.

The restaurant sign advertised a prime rib special for thirteen bucks, I was looking forward to it. The special started at five o'clock. There were twenty tables in the place, only three were occupied, and guess what... the special sold out. Fuck. "I'm sorry," the server says with a sad look on his face, "there's no prime rib left," well, what the fuck. How the hell can you be out of the advertised special in an hour, while there is no one in the place? There is no way it was eaten up that quick, we could have been cancer patients on our last meal. Anyways, I ordered chicken, Chief got a burger. The chicken was good, but not prime rib, however after two days of eating what seemed like cat food, it was good enough. Four hours later, I was hungry, I ordered the Asian salad room service. I was thinking that I might not get salads in Mexico for a few days, ya never know. Get something you can identify when you can?

The next morning, rested up and finished breakfast, we head towards the US Mexican border. It is a six-minute drive, but it makes people anxious. Three lanes going south open at seven am in the morning, not busy, just eight or ten cars in front of us. The US border security, seemed particularly vigilant, seemed they were looking for someone. They were checking people on the other side before they even crossed the Mexican border. A few SWAT guys looked like they were looking for someone in particular. Efficient, most agents waved through travelers unlike the retards you get at the US Canadian border. Through into the US booths, you then head to the right along a fence, then left turn towards the Mexican booths. We were scooted right through, parked, and got our Visas, then headed for the Federal tolled highway (1D) which runs along the ocean, it was a clear warm day and not much traffic. There are three or four tolls along this stretch, and it is an hour to get to Ensenada. Easy driving for motorcycles and just eighteen pesos, still worth it. We stopped at Starbucks in

Ensenada for morning coffee, all was good. Chatted to a local skipper about the weather, he had a great phone weather app. He knew there was a rain storm was coming through, luckily, we would miss it, Oh ya. Through the border no problems, Starbucks and missed the rain, not bad for only 8:20 am.

Getting out of Ensenada is a little more of an adventure then it used to be. There is more traffic, more lights, and people just don't drive the same south of the border. It takes a while to get used to it, to acclimate yourself. For an example, drivers will be swerving in and out of lanes, no signals, or they don't even work, no brake lights either. Second, every eighth or tenth car is obviously operated by a "professional race car driver' because he is clearly racing, weaving in and out, passing on the shoulder. I can only assume he is late for work just like the other fifty percent of commuters. My advice, when your working your way through traffic like this, just try to blend in. Get into a nice mellow pace in the right lane, as long as you're not being choked out by someone's vehicle with a blown head gasket, billowing smoke out of the exhaust and you have to pass, or your lips will start turning blue.

Then there is the action, it is everywhere and a bit distracting. On some parts it is like driving through the center of a circus. That's how I describe it, there is stuff going on all over the place, right and left, above and in front. Such as very colorful bright things moving in the wind. You get used to it but sometimes it gives me a headache. Over stimulation, I think. This day, we made it out unscathed and were heading out of town. There are a few stretches where it is less populated. The road clears up of traffic a bit. Then you will go through another small town. Watch for the topes, you will be cruising along sixty to eighty kilometers, and they'll appear out of nowhere, extending across the road four inches high, three feet wide. Then there are the side roads that run parallel to the main road, be sure to watch for cars coming and going from these roads, the drivers apparently do so without looking or perhaps they are looking and just go anyways, shit happens.

Thirty years ago, the area cleared up right outside of Ensenada, but now there is a small town, a scrapyard, followed by lower rental income areas, also small farming communities. The area is not as clean as it used to be, a little rougher looking, more run down, trash blowing around. These changes are probably due to the increase in the population. This pattern goes on and on and on.

But you will go by the odd town that has grilled chicken on the BBQ spit. If you haven't had outdoor grilled chicken in Mexico, you are missing something. They used to use skeet briquettes, now most use propane, still smells great though. They start cooking at mid morning and keep it going throughout the day. The smell causes me to salivate every time. We drove by the first two and missed a great lunch.

We stopped at the next town. There was a restaurant sign, so we ask if it is open, no restaurant here, but points down the street. So, we head down a side road, two more people standing in front of this restaurant. Ask if they are open, no. This is followed by another point across the street. Okay, maybe lucky on the third try? So, again we cross the street. Restaurant is open and we had a good meal. Tortillas, beans, rice. Buddy had a club sandwich, not sure why his meals always looks better than mine and he gets twice as much food. He is half my size, what the fuck.

The owner had worked in the US and moved from mainland Mexico for a quieter life. He said that not much happened here except farmers and cowboys drinking on Saturday night. The mainland was too crazy for him, he liked it here. He was always looking out the window, checking things out. Maybe he was in witness protection, or just twitchy. Nice guy though, had his daughter or a young girl working the front, he cooked. He asked where we were from and said he had been up to Vancouver and traveled Canada a bit. We finished up our lunches and headed back to the road.

Our goal that day was to make to Santa Rosalia. It was about half an hour before the area starts to clean up, a little less garbage blowing around, more undeveloped natural areas. Road was in good shape at the time. The bottom half of Baja California Sur is still cleaner and better organized. Less bullshit, people still work for a living, more family oriented. Getting gas is important in Santa Rosalia, sometimes it is two or three hundred kilometers till the next fuel stop. Sometimes there are guys selling gas from pickup trucks without much of a markup. It is possible that it's stolen fuel. I know that's hard to believe. I have used it a few times without a problem. That was our first day in Mexico, the room was five hundred pesos, about $28 US. No air conditioning, just an overhead fan, and a courtyard. It was plain but did the job.

The restaurant down the street is famous with the score racers and the Baja 1000 people. Walls are covered in photos, stickers and motorcycle memorabilia. According to the locals, the woman who opened it and ran it for forty years had died at the ripe old age of 160 or 116 they weren't sure. Either age is quite impressive for Mexico. The food was good, and the tables were clean, beer was cold. I can see why the racers liked it. You need beer to get all that dust out of your throat.

There were a few groups of people at different tables all chowing down. The guy at the table next to us was by himself, all geared up for off road. His full off-road bike was parked outside. He looked like he had put in a few miles on that day. He was tired, run down and dusty, but content. He was in his 40s, been divorced recently and needed to clear his head. We started talking. He was marking the trail for the Baja 1000 rally, a four-day event. It was to start the following week. He had been scouting the trail markings on the GPS for three or four months, fifty days of off-road driving and he looked like it. If you have done off road riding, you will know that's quite a bit of riding for that period of time. He did have some sponsorship, but he also loved it and had done it for years, free. He showed us a video of when he was about to crack on a particularly hot day after dumping his bike a few dozen times. He was a little distraught in the video but laughed about it now and wouldn't trade it for anything. His phone started ringing, calls from the organizers, interesting guy.

We hung out in the courtyard at the hotel, drinking, bull shitting and listening to music. A couple of other hotel guys joined us after a while. They brought out some more beers, told a few stories of traveling the Baja, doing road trips once a year. One of the Mexican nationals had been sent off to a Victoria boarding school as a kid. He had good memories of Canada in the winter, skiing, hiking, girls. His family worked in shipping goods across the border.

Eventually the subject of massages came up again. Chief would bring up the subject each night. I am fine with that, but they are just hard to find if you don't know the town or the area. We've had this discussion several times. He still likes the idea. Me too, if we can find one. On the other hand, he's had prostate cancer. So, he can no longer get an erection. He had his prostate removed rather than go through chemo or radiation therapy, this is not unusual. We joke around whether or not the massage has a "happy ending."

He's like, "mine is not going to work anyways." Ha ha. "It's not going to hurt if they touch it either," I said.

You know uhh... Maybe you could get a blow job instead, of the handy. You know, they could just chew on it a bit.

"A little tongue, a little lip." He said, he hadn't thought of that.

I tell him it's not unusual to get a blow job when its flaccid. Here's an example, an old girlfriend of mine, she was a bit of a nymph. I would wake up in the middle of the night and she'd be down there giving me a blow job. I'm pretty sure when she started it wasn't erect, but by the time she finished it certainly was. He thought that was amazing, whatever happened to that woman. Hmm. Another time. She was a little too motherly.

Another girl I dated would jump right down right after regular sex when I had popped it out still wet and warm, she would just start chopping on it. Who am I to complain? Ya.

He's like, "no way, no way, that does not happen."

I go, "maybe you should have dated a little more before marriage. It does happen... maybe you should discuss that with your wife."

There're women out there that are okay with that. He just sat there smiling, chuckling to himself and would not even give me an answer. That was our discussion on finding a massage parlor that night.

We got an early start the next morning 7:30. No breakfast at a $28 hotel. There was an Oxo (corner store, like 7 11 in Canada) down around the corner. We pulled in and had a sandwich and coffee with the locals. Hanging around outside nodding or saying good morning. It was a small town, a grocery store, the oxo and a couple of hotels. One guy chatted for a bit, he had traveled up to Canada years ago. It always surprises me how much the guys running the taco stands had traveled. This guy in San Jose I met on a side road had traveled to Europe the year before with his wife in the off season. There must be some money in tacos.

We scooted out of town, it didn't take long to fall into the groove. Not much traffic in the morning, the air was cool, no wind, good riding. There are few small communities that at one time had gas stations in them, but for some reason they are now shut down. I'm guessing that there are so few people they just got robbed and stripped out. Probably wasn't worth it to keep the business open.

You can easily get lost in the desert's sunrises and sunsets. Their glow attracts your focus, the colors begin to enhance, becoming; brighter and sharper. Living objects appearing closer than they are. The wind and rumble of the engine fall from you like layers of dust. Until a hair pin curve comes along and brings you back to the here and now. Gearing down, then winding back up through the gears for the straight a way. What was I really looking at back there?

There's one region where you will find vast valleys littered with huge rounded stones. Some the size of small houses. Wind blown and ancient looking. As far as you can see in either direction. It's about a kilometer to cut through it. According to a geologist I met years ago, it's part of an ancient river bed from when the Baja was attached to the mainland, possibly millions of years ago. Either way it's impressive.

Then you are back into rural villages and winding hilly roads with long flat straight stretches. On a sport bike you can open her up, but on a R1150GS you are at 80 to 110 km an hour. They don't corner as well as a sport bike. I like this section of the Baja. It quiet, less fussy. You can see things coming. If you screw up it's usually your own fault.

CHAPTER 17: GUERRERO NEGRO

We arrived at Guerrero Negro by four in the afternoon. It hasn't changed much. One main strip and a few side roads. I took a few circles around town to find the same hotel I stayed at in '86. It is now painted white instead of brown. The old restaurant that was attached to the building has been turned into a suite. The courtyard is now unused and run down. Front office is operated by a dead eyed zombie rather than an owner. The price is right for an older style Mexican hotel. No not the same vibe as '86, but what is?

The eating is pretty good in Guerrero Negro. Like I said, they have had a lot or score racers and Baja 1000 guys come through here over the years. It has kind of an interesting history, it was an old salt mining town. They would flood the flats with sea water and let the water evaporate then harvest the salt. Besides that, it is a lot of flat nothing. We were recommended a restaurant across the street. Good food and pleasant staff. They had just opened up for the season a week earlier. It was a fairly early night with two old guys snoring away by nine pm... Well, for one of us anyway.

I hadn't planned to go out, it had been a long day. Buddy was already sleep when the itch came back. I wanted to check out that back road through the dump like I had in '86. I spotted it on the way into town. It was still there, still well used. I got dressed and geared up. Without waking him, I left the room and started the bike and found the switch for some extra LED lights I had installed. I had tucked the switch away behind the headlights. Heading out of town it was only about one kilometer before the dirt packed road. I checked the clock on the bike. I was going to keep it to a time frame of ten minutes max to find the old whore house. If it wasn't there or had shut down, I planned to turn around head back to the hotel. The road wasn't much different now than it was thirty-two years ago, just hard packed sand and clay. Nothing but litter and desert on either side. Not very inviting, but I wasn't invited. This was free will, going out into nowhere. Probably the place most people try and stay away from.

I had only traveled for six or eight minutes, but even by now, I couldn't see the lights from town or any lights period. The road also seemed to keep repeating itself every 100 yards or so, like I had kept driving the same section. over and over. I'm not sure how many times. Maybe it was my imagination, I must have been in a dip not to be able to see any other lights.

Sure, as shit I saw a building in the distance, left side of the road, there was a light. It looked like the same place, definitely a bar. There was another motorcycle parked out front and a couple of cars. The place had gotten busy. The motorcycle was similar to mine, a BMW. The hairs on the back of my neck were standing up. There was something strange about the short ride on that dirt road.

I shut the bike off and went into the bar. There were a couple of locals at two tables and a guy at a table by himself, minding his own business. As well as one bartender, looking bored. No girls appearing from nowhere this time. The guy at the table by himself looked a lot like me. I went over and sat with him. We eyed each other up and ordered some beers. He could have been my brother, or for that matter a twin. We introduced ourselves, we had the same name and we both seemed to know who we were. I said it had been quite a while since I last saw you. He said, "I've never met you before."

I told him that back in '86 on the Baja highway, we had met.

We rode on the same Suzuki GS1100S. He agreed that he had made that same trip thirty-two years ago, and he had passed a young man riding the same motorcycle, wearing the same clothes. But he had not stopped. He had thought about it, instead he just kept going. But now, "here you are and here am I."

We had a few more beers, talk was thinning out. Both of us seemed more distant this time. Nothing I could put my finger on. Maybe we were just older. I asked if he had any thoughts on how this shit could happen. He just said, "what he had read," the mandala affects, or the existence of parallel universes, much like myself. Could versions of our self's be continually slitting of from this reality. Is so how could we exist in the same dimension as we were now doing. This sure as shit doesn't happen to everyone, he said. Fuck it, lets have a rum or two. We talked about children, wives, good lays, and shitty jobs. He said he was going to hang around a bit longer. I was ready for bed. I left some money on the table and headed back.

Same old dirt packed road. Within a few minutes I could see the lights from town. I stopped and looked around. The bar lights were nowhere to be seen. I made it back to town and stopped to top up my fuel for the next day. The old guy pumping the gas spoke a bit of English. I asked him about the old whore house on the dirt road outside of town. He said there was one years ago, but it had been stripped away and torn down. I paid him for the fuel and headed back to the hotel. Buddy was still sleeping, just like me in a few minutes. I focused on the point between my eyes that usually instantly puts me in a dream state and helps me to fall asleep. I dreamt of flying and teaching kids and youths to fly, that is always fun. I woke up rested and clear headed.

Quick breakfast in the morning, before heading South. On our way out of town we passed the garbage dump, could not miss it, it is still there, on the east side of the road. There is blowing litter and plastic for as far as you can see. They used to use thin plastic to cover the juvenile crops, it keeps the moisture in. If these plastic sheets are not disposed of properly, that is what happens, it decomposes and blows around in the wind for fifty years. Looks like shit. The road that led out to the whore house back in '86 still looked well used, like the ladies. I never mentioned it to Chief, he would have just asked about the possibility of a massage and his Honda 1600 wouldn't have made it through the sand anyways. Now, I'm not sure how I did it on a fucking sport bike. But at 26 years of age, that shit was easy.

The last two days in a row the wind had been coming up thirty to fifty kilometers, usually sideways, starts beating you down after a while. If it is at your back, it feels like you are going twenty or thirty kilometers less than you are. That is good, feels like sailing down wind. Not so good in a headwind or side wind. So, odds are against a good wind day. You just dig in and grind your way through it.

Heading south past Guerrero Negro is identical to heading north. Straight as far as you can see. The electrical poles start to look like matchsticks going off into the morning haze. The smell of dew and evaporation from the cacti, flowers, and grass is ripe. The rising sun works the shade and pulls the mist from the ground. Cooling the air for a few hours each morning. It was good riding. My head was clear. A couple of hours later we pulled into a small town for gas and some food. My ass was developing some chafing after seven days and I was happy to get off the seat. There was a small palapa with some Corona chairs and clean tablecloths next to the gas station. We walked over and sat down. Nodded to the only other person in the restaurant. She said hello. She was in her late 40s or early 50s, a little weathered from the sun, but looked fit with a relaxed and alert look in her eyes. She looked familiar, but that happens a lot when I am travelling. Maybe I just look for familiar faces, who knows. I ordered mango fish tacos and mineral water, Buddy the same, but with a Pacifico.

She asked where we were headed about half way through our meal. She had given us a little time to chill out from the road.

We told her we were going to make it to Loreto that night. Then La Paz or push through to Los Cabo the next day. She said she was heading to Cabo herself. She does the trip every couple of years and planned to spend the winter down there. Working in the arts & crafts fairs. She was having trouble with her car, a Subaru Outback. It was a good vehicle, 4-wheel drive, but it had a small engine problem, not serious, but the part was going to take two days to get there, and another day to install. The exhaust gasket was leaking, causing the oxygen sensor to cut power. She might not make it up some of the hills if she continued. She had found a reputable mechanic in town. The local gringo car hauler had agreed to shuttle it into Cabo, within the next three to four days. She would cover his wage and bus fare back. She had booked a place to stay in Cabo and planned to catch the bus tomorrow. Jokingly, I said would she like a ride and that I only had my North Face duffel bag across the seat which could be moved to the back rack. That would give her room for a backpack and a few small bags on top of the luggage carriers. She smiled and said, "I was waiting for you to ask."

That was a bit of an unexpected. She was obviously adventuresome and apparently had ridden bikes through India and Thailand many times before. So, there was no problem. Damn, she looked familiar, her name was Rose, friends called her Rosie. We finished up our meal and Rose walked over to the garage where her car was. She talked to the shop owner and the car shuttle guy. Everything was set. She was very efficient and had not even grabbed a hotel yet in town. She left and came back twenty minutes later with one duffel and a backpack. To our surprise, we now had a passenger.

She didn't look too heavy which is good, maybe 130 pounds plus 30 pounds of gear. That won't make much difference to the R1150GS. It was hot, I was stripped down to a long sleeve cotton t shirt and jeans. I kept my riding boots and gloves on. I liked her tone of voice. I trusted her. Quickly, we were on the road. Her hands are wrapped around me. The passenger has a choice, round me or hands on the back rack. I like a woman's hands around me and a set of breasts pushing into my back. It feels good.

She was kinda feeling around once we were on the road. I think she was checking me out, maybe my fitness level or my muscle tone. Either one was okay with me. I had 30 years of judo and the same working in the trades. I still work out three or four times a week. The tone is still there. I don't get complaints. She pops her visor up, I was using the half helmet. She says, "you don't mind me checking you out do you." ... "Not at all, I'm liken it."

I was beginning to think she had worked as a masseuse. She was working my lats, traps and pecs, then onto my back and shoulders. Some masseuse some shiatsu. I'm liking all of this. Also, I should note that when a woman touches my thighs, even at 58 years of age, it just turns me on. A touch, a stroke above the knee. It's like electricity is running through me and she was working them. I was getting a chubby. This is getting to be up there with the top ten rides. I'm starting to slow down a bit, thinking about other things besides riding. Who wouldn't? Now Buddy likes to race ahead, but I'm hanging back for the moment. He is a least a half a mile ahead and I'm okay with that. Chief can still see me on the straight a way. All is okay.

At this point I'm reaching back rubbing her thighs with my left hand, then reaching behind her ass and pulling it toward me. It was reciprocated. My chubby was now a full erection, she's working my crotch and it's getting tight down there. I was still in jeans and riding. She is grinding me from behind and working me up front. She obviously has an adventurous spirit, because she starts undoing my belt, followed by my button, then my zipper. This relieves a lot of pressure. No complaints from me at all. I am moving my hips at this point because I am into it, she is into it. You know that sex rhythm that you get in with at some point in your life with someone, whether its emotional or physical.

It is was going pretty well. She reaches down into my pants and straightens things out and starts working it. We are on a rural section of the highway, but I am slowing down, just doing the speed limit, about 80 km/hr. I am pushing up on the foot pegs to loosen the tension on my pants. I am almost standing. She is working it a little faster and faster. I have got to keep both hands on the handle bars because I am having trouble focusing. I am getting close to an orgasm. It felt like I was working two parts of my brain at the same time, shifting back and forth between logic and pleasure. I wouldn't say over stimulation, but it was up there. I was multitasking and the endorphins are pumping. I am not sure how many people have tried to have sex on a moving motorcycle, but it's up there, well past the mile-high club. Whether you're in your 20s or your 50s... it's good.

This was not her first time on a bike. She finished me off. I am nodding and telling her that that was pretty good. She then tucked me back in, did up my zipper and button back up. A few more seconds and my belt was on. All at 80 km/ hr. Now I am not saying it's not messy, but it dries out fast, just a few stains as happy reminders.

Oh, I should mention the old guy in an old beat up farm truck. He looked about 70 years of age. I had made eye contact at about 100 meters out. He drove by us at the height of the action. I could see he wasn't sure about what the hell was going on. Then comprehension and a smile and a nod as he drove by. I was sure he was going to have a good story over some beers with the buddy's tonight.

I had a tank bag with some water in a camelback. I put the throttle lock on, and I pulled it out, things were washed up. Hands too, the front of my shirt got washed down, then tucked in at the front so it doesn't blow up to my armpits.

She was impressed I could do that with no hands. I said, "she was pretty good with her hands also," and that I enjoyed it, she replied she was hoping I would. Well who the fuck wouldn't. There was a good quiet vibe after that, like when a cat is laying on your chest, purring kneading you with its claws, staring into your eyes. Now, I couldn't see her eyes, but that's what it felt like. It felt like mutual attraction. Some sort of primeval scene. Something was going on just beyond the logical mind. It was as if we had known each other for years.

I started to pick my speed again and caught up to Chief within a few minutes. He had missed quite a show, unlike the old rancher. We got into Loreto an hour later and as usual we had to drive around in circles to find the Malecon, a strip of road and walkway right along the water. Loreto is a bit of a prawn trap, like La Paz. Once you're in town you cannot see the water.
Lots of restaurants, hotels, and a few shops. With helpful directions from the locals we were on the Malecon. We drove up and down a few times before we picked a hotel, the Oasis. We booked in and my passenger Rose said she would like a room for herself. Me and buddy were okay sharing one, on account of, we are cheap. We had all decided to have a snooze for a bit, then meet up for dinner and walk around town. Later after we had all cleaned up and put some lighter clothes on, we walked the strip to check on restaurants and prices.

We ended up coming back to the hotel, which had a good write up and okay prices. We ate a nice dinner on a terrace by the beach, under an old canapé tree with lanterns hanging from it. Good conversation and company, no talk of what happened earlier. We all agreed on a walk around old town, a few blocks away. We all felt sore from the riding. When Chief brought up the subject of massages, as usual. Our new friend Rose said, "she wouldn't mind one herself."

The locals pointed us a few more blocks down the road towards town and assured us with a smile that there are masseuses, working and open. We found the shop and they had four tables with light curtains between them, all open. Three masseuses looking for work. All were females, with lots of experience. 500 pesos for an hour. I went for the deep heavy massage. Most people can't handle these, but I have old injuries and liked the scar tissue to be broken down, so I wanted it heavy, my masseuse was in her thirties and look fit. So, I stripped down, most massages are done in the nude with a clean sheet on the table and another on top of you. Usually they check out your muscle tone in a few areas to gauge what you can handle. When they push in deep with their elbows, which is when I just start purring.

She started on the calf regions, mine are like tree stumps from thirty years of judo. She is working them up and down, then progressing back to up my shoulders and neck. Then, working further down my back, almost laying on top of me as she is working it. Her hands are moving down my spine between my ass cheeks to the crack of my ass then over my buttocks to the inside of my thighs. I like this. Holy fuck. Now I am still under the covers, but I have no clothes on. She wasn't shy and neither was I, we are both adults.

Then she refocuses down to the legs and starts working my calves again. This time going over my calves sliding up to my thighs, her thumbs moving up around my balls, or I mean ball. I only have one due to a bicycle accident as a kid. Everything still works normally, thank God, then up the crack of my ass. I am on my second erection which she starts working at the head of my body, without missing a beat. This seems to go on and on. I was not complaining. She moves back to my neck and shoulders. Heavy thumbs from between my shoulders to the back of my skull, then working my shoulders up to below my ears, back and forth. Before long, she heads down again to the calves, up and down up and down all the way. My cock is just tingling at this point. She asked me to roll over, time for the other side. I do as I am told. A nice agile role, the upper sheet hardly moves. She moves up to the front lifts the sheet and has a looked underneath. Smiles and says he looks like he's enjoying himself. I said," yes he certainly is, and he is very happy, mi gusto". If I were a younger man, I would have come on the sheets already.

Lying on my back, she starts on my shoulders, arms and chest. Then adding more oil to her hands, leans over me starts running her hands down my chest, massaging my abs, around my scrotum to my inner thighs, up and down up and down. I am sure she was just about getting poked in the eye each time. I wasn't sure how much more I could take. She says, "he likes this very much." Well yes, he does. A five-hundred-peso massage, wow I couldn't pay my wife to do this, believe me I have offered a few times. She laughs and tells me to pay for a massage, then hurry home, she will wait and maybe even leave some money on the counter for me. At this point I remind her it's not always about her. Then she usually says, "that's right it is about you huh."

My masseuse was then back down at my feet which are also as tight as rope. This gives the guy downstairs time to relax and distracts him. Who doesn't like their feet rubbed? She starts working the front of my legs up the thighs, right to the balls. Now he's up like a post again for maybe the four or sixth time. I have lost count and he's getting used to it. She moves back up to the front, leaning over me smiling, she says, "happy ending?" I say, "is it included." She smiles and say. "no 200 pesos extra or 12 dollars," will be extra nice and quietly so the people four feet away cannot hear. I said agreed, but I tell her, I had only brought money for the massage with me, "could I bring it by later?" with a smile, and some pleading in my voice. She said no with a wink. I said, "but look at me, I can't even walk like this." With the same smile and a mischievous tone in her voice said, "come back later."

I wiped the oil off, got myself dressed, gave her a hug and walked back to the hotel with my friends on that warm Mexican night. None of us spoke. Hell, we could barely walk. Damn my balls were aching. That was the best fucking massage I have ever had in my life. Nothing has come close to it. We all made it back to the hotel. I had planned to have a short nap then head back out for the happy ending. I slept till eight am the next morning, along with the others. I dreamt of sitting at a table of three, one person I knew, the other two were an introduction, we shook hands and came to a mutual agreement. The plan was to create something. I don't remember what.

We were all still quiet over breakfast with a little discussion about a quality of the massage. There were no complaints. I didn't mention my balls were still aching. It was my secret. We finished a light breakfast because we weren't feeling too hungry and packed up our gear at the Oasis. Then we were back on our bikes, Buddy, Rose, and I. All still not moving too fast, still feeling that "good sore" from the massages. Even if you choose a medium intensity massage, they still dig their elbows and thumbs in, some use the bones of their forearms. You will feel the massage effects, the next day when done properly, a good feeling. We get ourselves out of town. There is a winding section through the hills when your heading south out of Loreto, it takes about an hour to get through. Great on a sport bike, but a little clumsy on an older 1150 GS. After that, it is flat, wide open. Great riding, usually cool, no wind, no traffic, just crank it up and hide behind the windscreen.

We went through Insurgents, a farming community, then through the town of Constitucion. We made great time, within four hours we were outside of La Paz. That is a productive day. We had averaged between 100 km/hr to 120 km/hr. The road was in good shape, straight, no river beds with surprises, and very few animals on the road. We had pulled over and gassed up before La Paz.

We made the decision to push through to San Jose. Now, La Paz like Loreto, is a prawn trap. Both the city section and the hotel section are spread out along the bay which is shaped like a half moon. It is very easy to get disorientated. When you are looking at the water you tend to think you are facing east, but you might actually be halfway around the bay, so you're looking almost west. This causes you to drive into the sun, which is the wrong direction.

I do not know if it was shit ass luck, but both Buddy and I, remembered to make a right turn after the Walmart or Home Depot. This road runs along the dry river bed and heads in the right direction. Most times I have missed it, not this time, very unusual. Normally you can get caught in the prawn trap for half an hour or forty-five minutes. Some people may just give up and get a hotel. Not us, not this trip. After taking the right along the river bed, within two kilometers we made a left, followed by a right onto the Mexican number one highway. This was a personal record for getting through La Paz.

Super Pollo is just what it sounds, more than enough chicken for a hungry guy. We ate a late lunch. Best chicken I'd had in weeks. Then took a visit to the banjo. Not much diarrhea this trip. Always a good sign when traveling through Mexico. Quick check over of the bikes and tighten the tie downs. We were on the road again for San Jose Del Cabo, oh boy. The road west out of La Paz is a straight four lain. There is not much around to see once you are out of town, within twenty minutes or so. There are a few bridges and curves, but not much else. On a sport bike or car, you could keep speed at 120 km/hr to 140 km/hr most of the way. It is fast driving but not what I would call good driving. There is a bypass route towards Toto Santos, so you don't see the town, but it is worth stopping there for a visit, if you have not seen it in a while or if it is a first-time trip. Following Toto Santos is a small community Pescador, more gas in Pescador and ninety kilometers to go and my ass was ready to tap out.

Pescador is followed by Cerritos beach. This is a great place for surfing or body surfing. This area is less developed then the corridor through Los Cabos. During this portion of the trip, every once in awhile, I had to check that Rose was still back there, she was good on a bike and had taken to leaning back on the rear pack. Chief took the toll road to San Jose. Rose had a place booked on the corridor, so we took the old ocean road. I dropped Rose off at a condo she had rented, gave her a hug and a peck on the cheek. We said we should keep in touch but did not exchange info. She was a free spirit and moved through the world as such.

As I was driving the last twenty kilometers to my final destination, I finally remembered. It was in '86, the stop I made in Oregon just north of Portland. Her name was Rose or Rosie Silver. Now that's a full circle, I wonder if she knew?

Disclaimer

This is a work of fiction. Loosely based on a motorcycle trip done in 1986. Then re-driven in 2018. Names, characters, businesses, places, events, locales, and incidents are either the products of the author's imagination or used in a fictitious manner. Any resemblance to actual persons, living or dead, or actual events is purely coincidental.

Front Cover Image Discloser

"image: Freepik.com". This cover has been designed using resources from Freepik.com